A SCANDALOUS PORTRAIT

ROSE ROOM ROGUES ~ BOOK ONE

CALLIE HUTTON

ABOUT THE BOOK

The Earl of Huntington (Hunt) is a silent partner in a successful gambling hell run by his two brothers. A well-respected member of the ton, he moves about in Society as an unknown agent for the Crown on its most sensitive matters.

Lady Diana is a long-time friend of Hunt's with the ability to embroil herself in difficult matters that require his assistance. Once again, she needs his help, but this situation could be a major scandal if discovered.

Against his better judgment, Hunt agrees to her scheme, but this time the circumstances cause him to see the woman he'd always considered just a friend in a different way. The strong attraction he feels must be squelched since she would never do as his Countess. Scandal follows her every move.

1

April, 1891
London, England

A glass of warm champagne dangling between his fingers, Sebastian, the Earl of Huntington, known as Hunt to family and friends, inwardly groaned as he studied Lady Diana Pemberton, daughter of the Marquess of Rockingham, as she single-mindedly made her way across the Billingsley ballroom, headed in his direction.

Dressed, as always, in the height of fashion in a rose-colored gown, trimmed with deep rose and green flowers, Lady Diana wore a frock that was low enough in the neckline to entice but not cause too many raised eyebrows among the self-appointed guardians of *ton* virtue. Her curly golden blonde hair had been swept away from her heart-shaped face to cascade down her back in a riot of bouncing curls. Leave it to Diana to eschew the dignified topknots and chignons the other young ladies sported.

As attractive as she was with that sweet face and mass of hair, her remarkable appeal lay in her wide-set crystal blue eyes framed by unusually dark lashes for a blonde. One had only to study those eyes to know every thought in Diana's head. There was no subterfuge or coyness about the woman.

Although slender was the current fashion, Lady Diana's full bosom and child-bearing hips made the other young ladies appear spindly in comparison. The gentle sway of said hips as she moved across the room hid the true woman beneath the façade of demureness.

Lady Diana was anything but demure.

He studied her covertly. As usual when he spotted her, his heart gave a thump, and his male part rose from its slumber. Yes, she was anything but demure and she was trouble, but for some reason his body was not in sync with his brain. She also captivated him with her high spirits and wicked sense of humor that sometimes bordered on the improper. Another way she was unique and quite different from other young ladies.

She wended her way through the throng with dogged determination, barely acknowledging the young men who attempted to gain her notice. Her steely resolve did not bode well for him. He'd known Diana for years and, over time, he'd had the unfortunate task of rescuing her from one disaster after another. He had gotten into more predicaments than a room full of toddlers due to the young lady headed in his direction.

He tried, somewhat unsuccessfully, to convince himself that it was merely memories of mishaps avoided, and disasters averted, that caused his muscles to tense and his heartbeat to quicken. His usual response to Lady Trouble. He continued to dismiss any other reason, despite the twitching below his waist.

"Ah, it appears we're about to have company." Lord Denning took a sip of champagne and nodded at Diana, now only about ten feet distant.

Both men straightened as she stopped in front of them.

"Lord Huntington, Lord Denning, may I wish you a good evening?" She gave a slight curtsey. Two pairs of male eyes assessed her neckline where it dipped as she did. Two generous creamy globes spilled over the top of her gown, moving more of Hunt's blood supply south. Also causing him to glare at Denning. "Close your mouth, man."

Diana rose and smirked, bringing a flush to Hunt's face at being caught ogling. The minx had done it again, put him on the defensive. One of her mischievous talents.

He bowed to her curtsey. "Good evening, Lady Diana. How was your visit with your family in Italy?"

After Diana had been caught in another tangle that could have resulted in a scandal, her father had hurried her off to some distant cousin in Italy where the girl had remained for a bit more than a year.

"It was quite pleasant, actually. I enjoyed my time there but am happy to be home."

She apparently did not wish to embellish that comment with stories, so he switched topics. That made things safer for him anyway. The less he knew about her adventures, the happier he was. "Are you enjoying your return to Society?"

She flashed him a brilliant smile, knocking the breath from his lungs. "As always. New ballroom, new gown, new hostess. However could I not enjoy it?"

He went on full alert at the look in her eyes. The vexing woman always tied him into knots, and this exchange was no different. How the devil was one supposed to respond to that cryptic statement? Instead of coming up with a smart, clever retort, which his befuddled brain was presently incapable of—most likely due to a lack of blood—he murmured, "Indeed," wincing inside at her raised brows and Denning's cough.

"If you will excuse me, Lady Diana, I fear I must

leave you both to your scintillating conversation as the orchestra is beginning the next set, and my partner awaits me." Denning made a quick bow, leaving Hunt to deal with the woman as he scurried off to the sound of instruments beginning a waltz.

"Coward," Hunt mumbled as the traitorous Denning took his leave.

Dancers gathered on the floor in the space allotted for dancing. Diana placed her hand on his forearm. "Dance with me, Hunt?"

He stared down at her, hating how she made him feel. Those blue eyes looked as innocent as she was not. Oh, he was certain that she was innocent in the right way of how a young lady must preserve her virtue for marriage, but aside from that, she was a problem looking for a place to set up housekeeping.

He felt as though he wanted to run as far from her as he could but only after he'd crushed her tempting body to his to show her that he was the one in charge; not her. He would not label her as manipulative, she was basically too sweet for that, but she did have a way of getting him to do things he preferred not to.

Despite his ability to run his estates profitably and speak in Parliament with aplomb and grace, his and Diana's lifelong relationship of push and pull rarely left him in charge when it came to Lady Diana. And now she wanted something from him. Of that he was certain. She always chewed her lower lip when she was ready to dump another problem in his lap.

He hated that he knew her so well, because that likely meant she knew him that well, also.

The privacy of a dance would provide her with an opportunity to embroil him in another of her scrapes. There was no doubt in his mind. Why he felt the need to constantly rescue her baffled him. They were no longer children, but she continued to turn to him, knowing with certainty that he would never let her down.

He'd had a peaceful year while Diana was in Italy, visiting her family and cooling her heels. Her banishment from the *ton* had given him many restful nights and a sense of order in his life. Thus far, he'd been able to avoid her since her return a couple of weeks ago. Rude, perhaps—he should have called on her—but his sense of self-preservation was strong.

Whether he was reluctant to be dragged into another disaster or merely happy to put his conflicting feelings about the girl on the shelf for a while, he had to admit he missed the chit.

However, seeing her now, with her impish smile and teasing manner that he knew was a prelude to asking for his help once again reminded him why he hadn't called on her since her return.

He'd been busy himself, since this Season he'd decided it was time to take a wife and set up his nursery. Hence the suffering he'd endured at numerous balls, garden parties, soirees, and dinner parties over the past weeks.

He had promised himself to take a serious look at the current crop of debutantes and see if any of them appealed. Unfortunately, none had gotten past his initial contact of a dance, dinner partner, or introduction from a determined mama.

He'd almost caught an ague from all the eyelash fluttering, and if he had to hear just one more young lady exclaim over how talented she was on the pianoforte, water colors, embroidery, and selecting just the perfect shade of ribbon to match a dress, he would abandon the idea of marriage and name his brother, Driscoll, as his heir.

"Of course, my lady. I would love a dance." He pulled himself from his ruminations and responded to Diana's question.

She smirked as he took her arm and led her to the dance floor. "You don't lie very well, Hunt. The look on your face tells me you would rather chew nails than dance with me."

Maybe not chew nails, but he would certainly prefer banging his head against the wall a few times.

He took her in his arms and experienced a shiver he'd oftentimes felt when this close to Diana. Like an electric jolt. The softness of her body, the musky, mysterious scent that was only her, and the way her blue eyes sparkled with merriment, as if she knew what sort of an effect she was having on him, all added to his discomfort. He refused to question it, preferred not to think about it, and pushed whatever it could mean to the back of his mind.

The very last thing he needed in his life was an attraction to Diana. Or, God forbid, a lifelong commitment.

"I had hoped you would call on me after I returned from Italy." She viewed him with mirth as he led them through an intricate turn. No pouting or sulking for Lady Diana. Everything was always straightforward with her. Instead of frowning, she regarded him with laughter. Most likely because she knew why he'd been avoiding her.

Despite the music and various conversations in the room, her familiar, melodious voice carried easily to him, sliding over him like warm honey. He couldn't help but wonder if that was how her mouth would taste. Then he mentally shook himself. 'Twas always best to be alert when dealing with Diana, not distracted by her appeal.

Before he could respond with something believable, she chose to discontinue that stream of conversation and said, "Will you call at my townhouse tomorrow afternoon? Say about two o'clock?"

Ah, he knew this was coming. "What have you done now, dear girl?"

She had the nerve to huff at him and raise her chin. "I have no idea what you mean."

If he wasn't so terrified at what her newest entanglement meant for him, he would have laughed at her righteous indignation. Surely, her memory was not that addled.

Her guileless look was greeted by his own aristocratic raised brows. "Given your history, my lady, my question is, unfortunately, appropriate."

She sighed as he pulled her close into another turn to avoid Lord and Lady Hanson. Once past the couple, he was reluctant to release her. She stared at him, but the slight pink tint to her cheeks told him she was aware of how their closeness had felt. "Will you come or not?"

There was no point in dithering since Diana with a request was like a dog with a bone. She never gave up. "Of course. I will be honored to call upon you and be of service."

Liar. I would rather shave my face with a blunt, rusty razor.

She grinned, which immediately raised alarm bells. Perhaps it was the year's absence, but in the short time they'd spoken, this newly-returned-to-Town Diana had evoked more conflict within him than all the years he'd known her. And that was certainly a frightening thought.

"Thank you." She smiled and dipped her head.

They finished the rest of the dance in typical useless chatter. Once he escorted her to her chaperone, he bowed. "Have a pleasant evening, my lady."

She tapped him lightly on the arm with her fan. "Have a pleasant evening as well, my lord. I look forward to your visit." She sashayed away as if she knew his eyes followed every move her delectable hips made.

Which they did.

Bloody hell. What was he getting himself into this time?

2

Diana breathed a sigh of relief as she made her way through the crowd and headed to the front door. Hopefully, it wouldn't take long for her carriage to be brought around and she could leave this blasted place. She grew more and more weary of these events as the Season wore on. Her feet hurt, the room was far too warm, and the beginnings of a megrim teased the back of her head.

She'd finally been able to take a deep breath when she spotted Hunt across the ballroom. For someone who was rumored to be searching for a bride this Season, he'd not been easy to run down. It seemed every event she'd attended, he was somewhere else.

"The carriage is ready." Her companion and chaperone, Mrs. Rachel Strickland, waved to her from the front door. Someday, she really must take the woman in hand and instruct her on proper behavior. One did not wave and shout across the entrance hall like some sort of fishmonger touting her wares. Diana's grandmama, Lady Priscilla Abbottt, had been exacting about good manners and would have been appalled.

She smiled every time she remembered her grandmother. Grandmama had been notorious in her time, which led Diana to believe she'd inherited some of the woman's infamous traits. Lady Priscilla Abbottt had been well-known throughout Polite Society for her shocking beliefs in equality for women and had held meetings on a regular basis espousing such outrageous ideas based on the writings of Mary Wollstonecraft and the scandalous Lady Caroline Lamb.

Lady Abbottt had indulged in scandalous affairs and, over the years, she'd broken several hearts. There had been quite a bit of grieving from the men of the *ton* at her passing.

And relief by their wives.

Diana held onto the footman's arm as she descended the slippery steps from the Billingsley townhouse and entered her carriage. A light drizzle had turned the pathway dangerous, and her dance slippers held no more purchase than stockinged feet. However, the coach was warm and dry, and she settled comfortably across from Mrs. Strickland.

She thanked God every day for the substantial fortune she'd inherited from her grandmama so that marriage was not something with which she needed to concern herself to maintain her comfortable lifestyle. Diana had not espoused Grandmama's ideas about no marriage and taking lovers instead, since she would like a family one day, but so far no man had tempted her enough to give up the freedom she enjoyed as a wealthy, unmarried woman.

Diana leaned back on the squab and closed her eyes to rest her head. At least the first part of her plan had worked. Despite his reluctance, Hunt had agreed to call upon her the next afternoon. Not that she'd expected him to decline her request. He'd always helped her in the past.

In fact, when she'd departed for Italy the year before —running from another potential scandal—he'd helped make the arrangements and had seen her off with his blessing. She tried not to be annoyed by his elation at her departure.

Lord knew she could not afford another opprobrium. Papa had already washed his hands of her and one more mishap would likely encourage him to send her to one of his far-flung estates near the Scottish border. It annoyed her to no end that even at four and twenty, he maintained control over her person. Thank God, not her money, though.

THE FOLLOWING AFTERNOON, Diana dipped her fingers into the blue-tinted powder box holding her Pear's Almond Bloom, the little bit of makeup she allowed herself. She rarely used it, but with the dark circles under her eyes giving testimony to her many sleepless nights since *the problem* had arisen, it kept her from answering countless questions from nosy matrons about the state of her health.

She'd always been outside the inner circle of young ladies who did everything they were supposed to do to maintain their standing with the *virtue vultures,* as Diana had tagged them. Those were the older ladies who set the standard for young girls' behavior. While never being given the cut direct by those ladies, they certainly did not view her with warmth or welcome her with open arms.

She checked the small pink and white flowered china clock on her dresser. It grew close to two o'clock. With her stomach in knots, she descended the stairs in search of her lady's maid, Marguerite, to act as chaperone when Hunt visited. Even though he was an old childhood friend, she did not want any sign of impropriety. She'd given Mrs. Strickland the afternoon off, since Diana did not trust her as she trusted Marguerite, who had been with her since she'd made her come-out four years before.

Plus, Marguerite already knew about the humiliation looming on the horizon. "Marguerite, Lord Huntington will be here momentarily. Please have Cook send in tea once he arrives, then join us in the drawing room so there will be no talk of us being alone together."

Tea, indeed. What she really needed was a glass of sherry, or even brandy, but it was necessary to keep her faculties if she wasn't going to make a complete cake of herself.

"Yes, my lady." The girl curtsied and hurried to the kitchen.

Diana wandered the drawing room, picking up objects, not really seeing them, then placing them back down, trying her best to calm herself. If Hunt refused her plea for help, she had no idea what she would do.

Her head jerked up and her pulse jumped, butterflies taking up residence in her stomach. The echo of a horse riding to the mews behind her house announced the arrival of her guest. *Just be calm. State your problem and appeal to his sense of duty and honor, on which he always prided himself.*

Within minutes, a knock sounded at the front door. Her butler opened the drawing room door and stood aside to let her guest enter. "His lordship, the Earl of Huntington, has arrived, my lady."

"Thank you, Briggs."

She sucked in a breath as she beheld the man she needed to save her from ruin. Tall—indeed much taller than he seemed in the ballroom last night—his presence overwhelmed the space in her drawing room. His thick, light brown hair, known for its inability to be tamed, fell over his broad forehead and teased the back of his cravat.

No tailor needed to pad his chestnut sack jacket,

which his broad shoulders filled out nicely. His deep tan trousers below a snug brown and black checked waistcoat outlined well-muscled thighs. A starched white pristine shirt set off his slightly tanned skin.

He'd gone from the gangly youth who had plucked her from trees and tended to her scrapes to a man who knew his place in the world and commanded a good part of it with aplomb and a touch of arrogance.

He offered a slight bow. "My lady."

She waved to a chair in front of the fireplace. "Won't you have a seat? I am expecting tea any moment."

She hated how breathless she sounded but convinced herself her disquiet was due to what she was about to reveal, not from his overwhelming presence. Had he truly been so very masculine prior to her trek to Italy? She attempted to remind herself this was Hunt. Her childhood friend.

And savior.

No sooner were the words out of her mouth than the door opened and Michael, one of her footmen, entered. He carried a tray with her favorite tea things that she and Grandmama had used for years. Alongside the lovely blue and while teapot sat a plate of small sandwiches and another plate of tarts. She gestured to the table between the two chairs, where the footman placed the tray. Her lady's maid, Marguerite, slipped into the room and took a seat near the door.

With shaky hands, Diana poured the tea, adding cream and sugar as was Hunt's wont. Once they were settled and initial pleasantries had been exchanged about the offerings on the tea tray, she placed her teacup firmly in the saucer and stiffened her back. "You must be wondering why I asked you to call."

He nodded, a slight smirk on his lips. "What trouble are you in now, Diana?"

She jumped up, causing him to quickly put his

teacup down and stand, the serviette on his lap falling to the floor.

"No, no, sit, please."

He offered her a bemused smile. "You know I am unable to sit while a lady stands."

"Oh, for heaven's sake. All right, I'll sit." She returned to her chair and then fidgeted so much she annoyed herself. She took a deep breath and smiled. "I learned about your rescue of Miss Manchester last month."

"Miss Manchester? Rescue? I'm afraid I do not understand." He picked up the teacup and frowned, obviously feigning ignorance.

"Perhaps you did not see it as a rescue, but I'm sure Miss Manchester felt it was."

He continued to look perplexed until she wondered if perhaps Marguerite had gotten the story wrong from Miss Manchester's lady's maid. Please, God, don't make it so. She needed Hunt's help. Desperately. "You seem confused, so perhaps I may refresh your memory?"

He nodded. "Please, do."

"The information I received was Miss Manchester was present at a house party where you were also a guest." When he continued to stare at her, she sighed. "Hunt, for heaven's sake, you are nowhere near your dotage. Did you or did you not attend a house party at the Bedford estate last month?"

"Yes, I did." He dragged the words out, his eyes narrowing.

"Was Miss Millie Manchester also a guest?" She tried to keep her voice calm, but the entire situation had been unnerving her for a week, and the sooner she could get his promise to help her, the happier she would be.

"I believe she was, along with her brother, Mr. David Manchester." The caution in his words was telling. A man protecting a woman's reputation.

Perfect. The sort of behavior she desperately wanted to encourage.

"If you are trying to guard the young lady's name, I admire you for that, but I assure you I know the story of how she left her scarf in a young man's bedchamber and, at her behest, you retrieved the garment for her before her brother discovered her indiscretion."

If he'd been surprised at her knowledge of the event, he did not show it. Instead, he viewed her with curiosity. "If you are in possession of that story, it has not come from me. May I ask why you bring it up now, and how that connects to the reason you have requested my presence this afternoon when I would much rather be on the way to my club? Are you missing a scarf, also?"

Once again, she hopped up and Hunt followed, spilling tea on his shiny shoe.

Diana sighed. "We are getting nowhere. Will you escort me to the garden? I think what I have to say would be easier if I am on my feet." Anything would be easier than the two of them jumping up and down like a couple of court jesters.

He hesitated a moment and glanced at the door as if considering making a dash for it. Eventually, he sighed. "As you wish."

He extended his arm, and they strolled out the French door, into the garden, Marguerite keeping a respectful distance behind them. The scent of bay rum wafted from him, temporarily distracting her. The muscles under her fingertips flexed as he maneuvered her around the flower beds. Goodness, he was warm. Heat radiated from him in waves.

You are stalling, Diana. Get on with it.

The time had come. No more hesitation. This needed to be done. She stopped in the pathway and turned to him. She raised her chin. "I have a favor to ask of you."

His slight smile gave her courage. "Ah, so now we've

come to the crux of the matter. Due to your nervousness, I assume you are once again in deep trouble. What do you want from me now, Diana?"

She took a deep breath and said, "I need you to steal a portrait from Mr. J. D. Mallory's art studio."

3

Hunt stared at Diana for almost a full minute. "I'm about to ask you to repeat what you just said, except I'm afraid I heard you right."

"Um. Yes, you most likely did. So, what do you say?"

His mouth opened and closed a few times. "No. Absolutely not." He backed up and, after a moment, he bowed. "I will leave you now." He stalked off before Diana even had a chance to say a word.

Stunned, she shook her head in confusion and stared at his retreating back with her mouth open. After a moment, she gained her senses and raced after him, almost losing her footing as her slippers slid on the carpeted stairs. Attempting to catch her breath, she looked around the empty entrance hall. "Did Lord Huntington leave?"

Briggs bowed. "Yes, my lady. And he seemed to be in quite a hurry."

Quite a hurry, indeed. She gritted her teeth and quelled the urge to kick the door since his shin was nowhere near her foot. Except that would only hurt. Well, this had only just started. She had every intention of getting that portrait back, and Hunt *would* help her.

. . .

TWO NIGHTS LATER, Diana searched the St. John ballroom for Hunt. She'd gone to three balls the night before and, tonight, this was her second. She would run the man down if she had to find him at one of his men's clubs.

Or she might even be daring enough to demand entrance to The Rose Room, the exclusive and extremely popular gambling hell Hunt owned with his two brothers, Driscoll and Dante Rose. It was not well known that Hunt was involved in the business, since he was mostly a silent investment partner.

Hunt hated any sort of scandal attached to his name and an earl owning a gambling hell did not portray how Hunt wanted to be presented to Society.

But Diana knew, and she also knew he visited the place and consulted with his brothers, a few times a week, at the very least.

Only women of the demimonde and disreputable mistresses dared visit the establishment, but surely Diana could weather that scandal much better than the one currently hanging over her head. She might even throw all caution to the wind and visit him at his home.

Oh, she would find him. There was simply too much at stake this time.

Giving up on this event, she decided to return to the entrance and request her carriage brought around, most likely to the displeasure of her chaperone who hated being dragged from place to place, but that concern was nowhere near as daunting as Diana's looming disaster.

There were two more events on her notecard. One soiree and one—she winced—musicale. Goodness, but she hated those things. But if Hunt was there suffering through it, she would too.

Diana was headed toward the corner where Mrs. Strickland sat with the other matrons and chaperones when Hunt's name was announced. She looked up to the top of the stairs.

There he stood in all his aristocratic arrogance, his eyes scanning the crowd and settling on her. He was dressed completely in black except for a white cravat tied in the most fashionable manner and a silver waistcoat. But more than the clothes he wore and how they fit was the manner in which he strolled down the stairs, aware, she was sure, of all the fluttering eyelashes, waving fans, and sighs coming from the young ladies watching him.

Handsome, titled, and wealthy, he was in the eyesight of many a desperate mama, as well as matrons and widows looking for one of the most sought-after lovers to warm their beds. A few began to move in his direction, but he merely nodded at the swell of ladies and made his way directly to Diana.

Damn her heart that sped up and her breathing that increased. It wasn't merely from fear of him rejecting her again as much as how he affected her. They'd been friends for years, for goodness sake. Why now did he turn her into a blubbering idiot when it was imperative she remain calm and simply use her well-honed skills to convince him to help her?

"My lady." He bowed to her curtsey. His serious mien was a contrast to the twinkle in his eyes. Good, maybe he would at least listen to her now.

"Good evening, my lord."

He extended his hand. "Walk with me."

He tucked her arm into his and moved them to the edge of the ballroom. Since it was still early in the evening, there was room for walking. Within a couple of hours, it would be almost impossible to move, let alone actually dance in the area set aside for such activity.

The bay rum scent from him as well as his fine-tailored, expensive clothing immediately put her body on alert. Aching nipples, rapid breathing and the butterflies setting up housekeeping in her stomach needed to be ignored. She must stay centered on what she needed from him.

"First of all, I must apologize." Hunt murmured the words but continued to face forward.

"Indeed?"

"Yes." He turned to her. "It was quite rude to leave your home the other day. 'Twas not well done of me." He grinned. "You do frighten me sometimes, Diana."

"Me?" She placed her hand on her chest, immediately drawing his eyes to her neckline. She dropped her hand and fought the heat rising from her middle. "Why would you be afraid of me?"

He pushed open the French door leading to the terrace beyond. The music started up, and several couples who were strolling in the garden and chatting on the terrace moved back into the ballroom.

Still awaiting his response, she let him move them down the few steps to the garden area, which was lit well enough to avoid scandal, yet sufficiently shadowed so that they would have privacy.

"You frighten me, Diana, because you've given me more than my share of sleepless nights." He raised his hand. "Before you begin huffing, please remember all the times I bailed you out of your messes." He smirked and looked down at her.

She must not be distracted by his rakish smile. Or his very male scent. Or his hooded eyes. Or the taut muscles under her hand. Let the other ladies swoon at his feet, she must keep her senses where he was concerned. "What messes?"

After a few moments, he said, "Must I number them?" He began to count on his fingers. "First there was the time you climbed a tree just as your parents' guests were arriving for a house party. If I remember correctly, you were stuck up there for hours before I found you."

"For goodness sake, Hunt, I was ten years at the time!"

"Ah. That is true. In that case, I will not number all the other rescues from then until you made your come-out." He turned them so they moved on the path around the side of the house where another set of French doors revealed couples waltzing by in the ballroom.

"Do you remember Lady Abercrombie's garden party?"

She offered a stiff nod.

"Do you also recall falling into the creek behind her house, drenching yourself, forcing me to sneak you out the back gate to my waiting carriage to get you home?"

"It was not my fault that the rocks alongside the creek were so slippery."

"Yet no other young lady took a swim that day." Hunt moved them to a stone bench under a tree, under a brightly lit torch. He apparently was not going to put them into a situation that would cause a scandal. At least nothing near what she was facing.

Once they settled, he took her hand in his. Improper as it was, since he was an old friend, she wasn't concerned.

"Then there was the time you took a ride on Rotten Row with the horse your papa forbade you to ride because the spirited mare was beyond your abilities." He gazed out into the garden, as if picturing the disaster that day. "If memory serves—"

Diana raised her hand. "Stop!" Whatever did the man do? Keep a list of all her indiscretions? She swore he was laughing at her.

He didn't seem annoyed at the recitation of her blunders but viewed her with amusement. "Therefore, Lady

Diana, since you appear to not want to hear the rest of my stories, I rest my case about the fright you trigger within me and the sleepless nights you have caused."

Diana took both of his hands in hers. "This is serious, Hunt. Not some mishap on a horse or falling into a creek. I am in serious trouble."

His amusement turned to something else. Something protective and, if she was wont to admit, possessive as well. "What happened, Diana? Did someone harm you? Do I need to call someone out?"

She shook her head and pulled her hands from his to hug her middle. "A little over a year ago—before I left for Italy, I arranged to have a portrait of myself painted." She glanced over at him. "As vain as that sounds, I did it merely to appease my late grandmother who had asked me for years to have a portrait done and hang it next to hers in the library at Waverly Manor, the estate I inherited from her, along with the London Townhouse.

"I was feeling quite blue and missing her dearly one day and decided to have it done."

Hunt felt a tightening of his stomach muscles, scared to death at what she was about to say. "Go on."

"I commissioned Mr. J. D. Mallory to do the portrait. I sat for him for hours, but I knew it would be worth it when it was finished." She took a deep breath. "At his insistence, he had me resting on a lounge, facing him, but with my head tilted in such a way that hair fell over part of my face, which was not clearly seen. I thought it odd at the time, but since I'd never had an official portrait done before, and didn't want to appear a novice, I merely acquiesced to his instructions."

* * *

Hunt studied her as she spoke, staring out at the garden, looking as though she wished to be swallowed up by the roses. He'd begun to realize she'd gotten herself into something deep this time but had no clue as to where her tale was leading. "Go on."

"He gave me the portrait before I left for Italy, and it is now hanging in the library at Waverly Manor." She stood to pace. "It is quite lovely, actually."

"Then what is the problem? If it's hanging in the library at Waverly Manor, why do you want me to steal a portrait from Mr. Mallory's studio? I don't understand."

Diana stopped and took a huge breath. "I've never spoken out loud about this, to anyone, but if you are to help me, I must trust you."

He reached out and took her hand again. "You know you can trust me, Diana."

She nodded. "Shortly after I returned from Italy, Mr. Mallory sent a note that he wished to visit with me at my townhouse in London." She turned to face him.

"Go on, sweetheart." Hunt stood and took her other hand in his. Even through both their gloves, he could feel her ice-cold hands.

Another deep breath. "When he called, he told me he'd made some changes to the portrait and would I care to see the difference. I was quite taken aback and confused to be honest, because I didn't understand why he would do such a thing. Or how he had even gotten it from my estate."

Hunt waited as Diana seemed to wrestle with something. He watched her, knowing she'd come this far, so whatever she had to tell him would eventually come out.

"At first I attempted to dismiss him, but he insisted he had the portrait in his carriage, and he wanted very much to bring it inside for me to see." She wiped beads of perspiration from her upper lip.

When she swallowed several times, he said, "Go on, sweetheart, just tell me."

"Thank goodness the portrait was covered in a sheet when he came back into the drawing room. He leaned it up against a chair and, once he had my complete attention, he whipped the sheet away."

All the blood left her face. and Hunt put his arm around her waist, certain he was going to have to catch her since she appeared ready to swoon.

"And?"

"It was my portrait, exactly as he painted it, but—" She chewed her lip until he was afraid he'd see blood. Then she blurted out. "I was naked!"

Then she covered her face and burst into tears.

J. D. Mallory is a dead man.

4

Hunt wrapped his arms around Diana as she sobbed against his chest. He was still having a hard time understanding exactly what happened and what else occurred after Mallory showed her the portrait.

It was the sort of thing, however, that Diana had to tell in her own way and in her own time. While he waited for her to compose herself and continue with the story, he planned several ways to kill Mallory. Hopefully the most painful way possible.

She accepted the handkerchief he held out to her and leaned back, wiping her cheeks and eyes. "Thank you."

Diana seeming somewhat calmer, he released her, and she sat back. Hunt took her hand again. "Tell me the rest."

Shuddering to take a deep breath, she fisted the handkerchief in her hands and looked at her lap. "I asked him how he got the portrait from my home, and he said he didn't, that this one was a duplicate he made when he painted the first one.

"Then he told me he had plans to sell the wicked portrait to a very wealthy client who wanted it but, considering my family's status, he would reconsider and sell it to me instead."

Hunt's blood continued to boil at the man's avarice and downright evilness. "How very considerate. And for a hefty price, I'm sure."

"Yes. He wants twenty thousand pounds."

Hunt almost fell off the stone bench. "Twenty thousand pounds! That's outrageous."

"Indeed." She offered him a slight smile. "That sum would also drain my accounts. For all intents and purposes, I would be left almost penniless."

Hunt's jaw worked as he considered the situation. To think with clarity, he had to push aside the tempting idea of racing to Mallory's gallery and pummeling the man. Even though, given what she'd just told him, it was apparent why she'd asked him to steal the portrait, he still wasn't sure that was the best solution.

"Can you not notify the police? The man is blackmailing you, and I am sure there is a crime he has already committed by painting a second portrait without your permission."

She shook her head vehemently, her eyes wide. "I cannot let anyone know about this. Word will leak, and I will be disgraced." She stood again and paced. "This is not some girlish caper I can recover from by escaping to Italy. With my reputation for the little bit of trouble I've already been in," she looked in his direction, and he quickly removed the smile from his face, "everyone will believe I actually posed for the portrait. You know how the *ton* is. Given the choice between believing the truth or considering what causes the most gossip, scandal wins every time."

"What if I went to the studio and talked to the man?" He had no intention of 'talking' with anything other than his fists. Once the problem was solved to Diana's satisfaction, Hunt still planned to beat the hell out of the cad.

"No. If he thinks there might be a chance that I won't pay him, or if I send someone on my behalf, he's already said he would turn the portrait over to the interested buyer." She threw her hands out. "And who knows what the buyer would do with the portrait?"

This was indeed a muddle. As she clearly stated, this was no minor infraction of a young girl pushing at society's strictures. Her life would be ruined, and her only recourse would be sinking to the level of the demimonde.

He would never allow that; despite all her 'adventures' Diana was a well-bred, innocent young lady.

Diana sat next to him and gripped his hands. "You must promise me that you won't tell anyone about this. Not even your brothers. No one. Promise me, Hunt."

He hesitated for a second. He'd just been considering asking his brothers for advice since he still didn't care for the idea of breaking into a studio and stealing something. "I promise."

She wiped her nose. "Now will you agree to steal the portrait?"

Hunt sat back and regarded her. "I'm still not comfortable with your solution."

"Do you have a better one? I cannot pay the man twenty thousand pounds. That's impossible. I will not turn over my entire life to him."

"I agree. But you must give me some time to consider our next step."

She smiled brightly for the first time in days. "*Our* next step?"

* * *

DIANA AWOKE the next morning with a sense of well-being that had been noticeably absent for the past week. Hunt was going to help her. She still believed the best—and possibly only—resolution was to remove the portrait from the studio and burn it.

She told Hunt that when Mr. Mallory came to her house with the portrait, he said he would give her two weeks, and then he would sell it. One week had already passed while she went around in circles trying to think of what to do, and then chasing down Hunt to help her.

She tossed aside those gloomy thoughts, along with the counterpane, and leapt from the bed. Marguerite knocked softly and entered the room. "Good morning, my lady."

"Good morning to you, as well. 'Tis a fine day, is it not?"

Marguerite crossed the room, opening the drapes. "You seem quite chipper this morning."

"Yes." Diana stretched. "I feel good. In fact, I believe I will take a ride to the park this morning. Can you ask Briggs to notify the mews to tack my horse? And I'll take one of the footmen with me."

"Yes, my lady. I will lay out your riding habit."

Feeling quite uplifted, Diana washed and dressed and sat for Marguerite to do her hair in a fashionable chignon. With one quick look in the mirror to adjust the feather in her hat that curled toward her lips, Diana smiled and left the room.

As if to match her mood, bright sun warmed the balmy morning air, casting a glow over the tree-lined street. Diana headed down the steps to where Charles, one of her footmen, held the reins of her Chestnut mare, Lady Poppy.

She loved the horse that was given to her by her father before he became more interested in his second family. Diana spent many hours flying over the hills at her estate, her hair streaming behind her as she flew over hedges. Of course riding in London was a bit more decorous, but it felt good to be out and about.

She fed Lady Poppy the apple she had in her pocket and ran her palm down the mare's velvet nose.

Once Charles helped her mount, he climbed onto another mare from her small stable, and they trotted down the road, turning right, toward Hyde Park.

She breathed in the fresh air and relished the warmth from the sun on her face. Grandmama would certainly chastise her for not keeping her face covered, but occasionally it felt good not to worry about maintaining her pure white skin.

Her good cheer dimmed a bit. Grandmama had been her chaperone and champion for many years, and every day without her etched another hole in Diana's heart.

Only a few months after Papa's second wife had taken over the only home Diana had ever known, Lady Abbott had arrived on Diana's doorstep, along with numerous pieces of luggage, trunks of books, and a small dog clutched snug against her side by a hand with more rings than fingers. She had swept past the butler and announced to the startled governess that she had come to raise her granddaughter.

Diana had hidden behind her governess's skirts, taking peeks at the formidable woman who smelled of roses and stood only a few inches above Diana. In a very loud and determined voice, Grandmama declared to anyone listening that, despite a new stepmother—she sniffed—she, and she alone, would see to the welfare of her only child's only child. It was years later that Diana learned Grandmama had never approved of the match between Diana's parents. More telling was the fact that Papa had not objected to the removal of his daughter.

Diana, Grandmama, and Diana's governess, Miss Blackstone, departed a few weeks later. Papa, and particularly the new Lady Rockingham, were not happy with the addition of the formidable woman to his household.

They then traveled to Grandmama's manor home, right next to Hunt's family estate, far from London and nestled in the lovely hills of Yorkshire, full of wild flowers, woods and snug cottages.

That was where she'd spent the next nine years before they returned to London for Diana's come-out, two years before Grandmama's death. They were marvelous years of learning, growing, exploring, and becoming the woman with whom she was quite happy and satisfied. All thanks to Lady Abbottt.

Lord, how she missed that woman! Lady Abbott had been eccentric and outspoken and loved her granddaughter to distraction. From the time Diana had arrived at her estate, she'd received more attention and care then she'd seen all the years under her parents' ministrations. Or lack thereof.

Pushing those memories from her mind, lest she turn maudlin, she and Charles began their ride on Rotten Row with a few others out for an early ride. 'Twas not usual to see members of the *ton* out and about so early since most would have attended some sort of social affair the evening before and arrived home barely before dawn.

She stopped and chatted with the few people they met and, after about an hour, feeling refreshed and ready to take on the world, Diana returned with her groom to her townhouse in Mayfair.

"Please ask Cook to send in breakfast. I am quite hungry, and I will be down as soon as I change my clothes." Diana spoke over her shoulder to Briggs as she made her way up to the bed chambers where Marguerite had already straightened her room and had her day gown laid out for her.

She loved the yellow, thin-striped, linen dress; 'twas one of her favorites. Marguerite added a bright yellow ribbon to her hair and, with a very unladylike grumble in her stomach, Diana entered the breakfast room.

Smells of savory sausages, eggs, toast and beans almost made her groan. She filled her plate with much more than she knew she would eat and poured tea.

"My lady." Briggs entered the breakfast room with a salver holding an envelope. "This came for you while you were in your bedchamber."

She wiped her mouth with the napkin and took the missive. "Thank you." She placed it next to her plate and eyed it as she took a sip of tea. She didn't recognize the handwriting, and it didn't appear to be an invitation. Shrugging, she pushed it aside and ate her breakfast.

After she was through reading the newspaper with her breakfast, a luxury many women did not have since in most households the husbands got the freshly pressed newspaper before his wife did, her eye was once again caught by the small cream-colored envelope.

She broke the seal and flipped the parchment open.

One week, my dear lady. My client is most anxious to take possession of the portrait.

The writing was bold and crisp. Nothing elegant or mannerly about the words or the confident strokes of the letters.

Diana tossed the letter down and took a deep breath. Her breakfast attempted to make a re-appearance on her lap.

Please, Hunt. You must get it back.

* * *

LATE THAT EVENING, Hunt entered The Rose Room, the club he and his two brothers, Driscoll and Dante, owned as a joint venture.

Driscoll was his full brother and Dante his father's

bastard who was raised with them. There was never a difference in the way Dante was treated by their father, but Hunt and Driscoll's mother made it known on occasion that Dante was not 'one of them'.

To Hunt, they were both his brothers, and he loved them as only brothers can. Over the years they fought, played, attended Eton together and vied for the same opera dancers.

Three years ago, Driscoll and Dante had come to him with a proposition to open a gambling hell. Hunt thought it was a good idea since, although he was prepared to provide for his brothers, he knew it would be a much more rewarding life for them if they had their own means of support. The ridiculous edict of gentlemen not working be damned.

Hunt threw in the financial backing, and he'd been well rewarded with their efforts since then. The club catered to the elite of London, the Upper Ten Thousand, and the newly rising wealthy merchant class. The only women permitted were mistresses and members of the demimonde. No true lady would ever step past the front door.

Hunt walked through the club, satisfied at how busy the tables were, and made his way upstairs to the offices.

His brothers sat at their desks, Driscoll's head bent, going over numbers in one of his numerous ledgers and Dante slouching, his feet on the desktop, snapping a rubber band.

"It's nice to see that at least one of you is working." Hunt knocked Dante's feet off the desk and leaned one shoulder against the wall, his arms crossed over his chest.

"We're working. I'm taking a break." Dante stretched and stood. "Now I'm about to go downstairs and mix and mingle. Encourage our customers to spend money."

What no one except the three of them knew was, while the gambling hell was the two younger brothers' true source of income, all three brothers took occasional sensitive assignments for the Crown.

With his low-key attitude and extraordinary way with numbers, Driscoll Rose was a trained agent who worked on the more difficult assignments that even the bravest of the brave shunned. Dante's lackadaisical attitude got him the reputation as rake, libertine, and *bon vivant.* However, the easy-going gambling hell owner possessed skills with his fists and knives, along with the ability to remain cool and calm in any situation that put him at the top of the Crown's list to call in when an assignment was about to turn sour.

Hunt, as the head of an old and respected family and title, had contacts among the upper class that provided the Crown with an inside agent when they had no other way to gain imperative information.

What the world saw were three brothers working together in a successful business, living the life of young, wealthy, handsome men who every debutante in London would welcome as a husband. Even the bastard son.

Dante opened the door to return to the gaming floor, then turned back to Hunt. "Did you hear about Lady Diana?"

Hunt's stomach sunk to his toes. Had word already spread about her up-coming disgrace? "What about Diana?"

5

Dante stepped back into the room and frowned. "What's wrong? You look angry."

"What did you hear about Diana?" The words came out more clipped than Hunt would have liked.

Dante shrugged. "Only that she is back from Italy."

Hunt let out the deep breath he'd been holding. "I know."

"Have you seen her?" Dante asked, still viewing him with a puzzled expression.

Although he would love his brothers' input on Diana's situation, he promised to keep silent about it, so he merely shrugged. "Yes. Briefly at the Billingsley ballroom the other evening."

"I heard she's looking quite dazzling." Dante winked.

Hunt's jaw muscles tightened. "What is that supposed to mean?"

Driscoll's jaw dropped as his brother looked up from his work and regarded Hunt with raised brows. "Blasted hell, brother, since when are you so touchy about Lady Trouble?"

"I am not touchy about Diana. And don't call her Lady Trouble." Damn, if he didn't shut his mouth soon, his brothers would start a lot of speculation and asking questions which he didn't need right now with her predicament looming over his head.

Also, it was highly unusual for him to be touchy about the girl. She'd been a thorn in his side for years, as well his brothers knew. Normally, he treated her with reserve, or at the very least, provided her with a wide berth.

Now the situation had shifted. He hated to admit it but, ever since their conversation, he'd thought about nothing except how she would look in the nude. Did she have pale or dusky rose, or deep brown nipples? Was the silk hair that covered her mound the same lovely shade as the hair on her head?

When he realized his body was beginning to react to his thoughts, he quickly switched the subject before his brothers noticed. "Didn't you say you were about to go back to work, Dante?"

"Yes. I did say that." Dante cast another bemused look at his brother and left the room.

Hunt pulled out a chair and sat, facing Driscoll. "How are we doing? It looks like a good crowd down there on the gaming floor."

His brother laid his pencil on the desk and leaned back. "Very good. We had to cut off young Wentworth last night. He is too far in debt and rumors abound that he has been selling just about everything at his estate not entailed."

Hunt shook his head. "What a fool. All that will get him is heavily into the market for a rich bride."

Driscoll smirked. "No doubt. Better keep him away from Diana."

Hunt stiffened. "What does that mean?"

Driscoll stared at him. "Damn, brother, you are definitely out of sorts when it comes to Lady Tr—"

"Don't. Say. It."

Driscoll raised his hands, palms up, in surrender.

"Personally, I prefer not to delve into whatever it is that's bothering you, big brother."

"There is nothing bothering me."

Liar.

"As you say. Are you here merely to keep me from my work, or do you have a purpose?" Driscoll tapped his pencil on his desk.

"No purpose. Just stopped in to have a chat with my brothers, but apparently my timing was off." Hunt headed to the door.

"Either your timing or your attitude."

Hunt saluted him with a rude gesture and left the room to the sound of Driscoll's laughter. He hurried down the stairs and decided a late-night drink at one of his clubs was in order.

White's was bursting at the seams which told Hunt most of the evening's balls, soirees and musicales had ended. Before visiting his brothers, he'd spent some time at the Manning come-out ball for their youngest daughter, but when he didn't find Diana there, he left after an hour.

Why it mattered to him that she wasn't there annoyed him since he'd gone to dozens of affairs in the time she was hiding in Italy and didn't miss her at all. Damn that portrait and the image he could not get out of his mind.

"Hunt!"

Hunt turned toward a small group of gentlemen, Lord Allenby waving at him. After instructing one of the footmen to bring him a drink, Hunt wandered in the direction of the group.

"I hear Lady Diana Pemberton has returned from Italy." Stephen Blackmoor, a long-time acquaintance since Eton, nodded at Hunt as he took a seat across from Allenby.

Hunt reached for his drink from the footman's tray. It would be Blackmoor who made that statement since the man loved gossip more than the old, disapproving matrons of the *ton.*

"Yes. She has." He sipped his brandy, hoping he was not going to have to speak all night about the woman of whom he was trying to rid his mind.

"I can't help but wonder what sort of trouble she's going to get into now?" Lord Belton grinned, and the others all nodded. Belton raised his glass. "Here's to another fine scandal in the making."

The others saluted him, but Hunt glared in Belton's direction. "It is not proper to speak of a well-bred young lady that way, Belton."

Belton gave him a dismissive wave. "Come now, Hunt. You can't think she will stay out of difficulty, can you?" He downed the rest of his drink and signaled the footman. "Of all people, you should know that. How many times have you played the knight in shining armor to her damsel in distress?"

"Maybe we should place a wager in the book," Talbot said, leaning forward. "How long it will take before she is in trouble again."

"If you," Hunt looked around the group, "if *any* of you, write Lady Diana's name in that book, or a book at any club in London, you will face the consequences at the end of my fists."

Shocked looks and silence greeted him. "Sorry, Hunt. Didn't know that was the way of things," Blackmoor said, his brows raised.

Hunt tossed the rest of his drink down, the burning liquid settling in his sour stomach. "There is no *the way of things.* I just won't allow a young lady of good breeding to be maligned in my presence."

When silence remained, Hunt placed his glass on the table in front of him. "Gentlemen." He rose and strode from the room. He was obviously not in the proper frame of mind for companionship.

Still unsettled as he rode home in his carriage, he

pushed aside the picture in his mind of Diana naked and reclining on a lounge, and instead focused on what he could do to help her.

Steal the portrait.

Once the carriage rolled to a stop in front of his townhouse, he jumped from the vehicle and addressed the driver. "John, when you return the carriage, please wake the groom and ask him to saddle my horse."

As a well-trained servant, the driver offered no reaction to his master requesting his horse saddled for a ride in the middle of the night.

Hunt bounded up the front steps and proceeded to his bedchamber. His valet, Marcus, awaited him.

Hunt began pulling off his cravat. "I need to change into riding clothes."

Also used to his master's comings and goings over the years, Marcus merely nodded and walked to the wardrobe where he extracted appropriate clothing.

If he were to attempt to sneak into Mallory's studio and swipe the scandalous portrait, he needed to first assess the place. Not that he was committed to stealing it. He just wanted to see what the possibilities were before he spoke with Diana.

Damn, the woman could get herself into the most trying situations. Finding herself in the dark part of Vauxhall Gardens with one of London's worst rakes had forced her flight to Italy. Of course, had she agreed to marry the Viscount Stratford as was expected in those circumstances, she would not have been forced to escape London under a shroud of scandal.

However, Diana being who she was, refused to marry the man, said he tricked her into being caught, was only after her money, and furthermore, she declared loudly to all and sundry that Stratford was an *arse*.

In those very words.

Now there was a naked portrait of her floating

around and, if it wasn't retrieved before Mallory sold it, her reputation would be unrecoverable.

Truth be known, this was one time Diana was truly not at fault. Her only crime was trusting Mallory, although she had no reason not to. His reputation as a respectable art dealer was unchallenged. He had chosen his victim wisely, knowing that Diana was without male protection, wealthy, and could not afford another black mark against her reputation. Being the greedy bastard he was, Mallory had asked for just about every pound the woman owned.

Dressed in appropriate clothing, Hunt swung his leg over his horse, a dark Irish Hunter, named—appropriately—Black Diamond, and headed to Albemarle Street where the Mallory studio was located. It was not a long ride and, with most events of the evening over, the streets were quiet.

He viewed the building from the front, then climbed down from Black Diamond and surveyed the outside of the place from all sides. He took note of the structures on either side. He strode up the steps and tried the front door, which was, expectedly, locked.

Back down the worn steps, he took a final look at the building and surveyed the area. His mind made up, he mounted the horse and headed home.

* * *

THE NEXT MORNING, Diana looked up from the book she was reading at Briggs entrance into the drawing room. "My lady, Lord Huntington has called."

"Oh, thank you. Please send him in." She quickly slid her feet to the floor where they had been tucked under her bottom. She bent to retrieve her house slippers and pulled them on. She closed her book and placed it on the table. Assured she was ready for this visit, she looked up with a smile as Hunt entered the room.

"Good morning, my lady." He bowed before her, and she extended her hand.

"Would you care for tea, my lord?"

My goodness, aren't we being formal, she thought, and held back the giggle that was about to erupt from her throat.

"No, thank you, I have just broken my fast."

Diana waved to the comfortable wing-backed blue and white striped chair across from where she sat. She hid her hands in her lap as they began to tremble. She knew by the look on his face that he had reached a decision about stealing the portrait. She briefly offered a prayer that he was willing to do it.

If he refused, she had no idea what she would do next.

"There is no point in dithering. The reason for my visit is to advise you that I have not come up with any other solution to your problem except for the one you have suggested. I need to steal the portrait from Mallory's studio."

Tears filled her eyes, and she released all the tension in her body. Her palms together in a prayer-like position, resting against her lips, she said, "Thank you, Hunt. You have no idea what that means to me." Her voice trembled, and she dabbed at the corner of her eye.

"I cannot allow Mallory to take every pound from you, or in the alternative sell the portrait to whatever client he has that wants it. I will be honest with you and admit that, in my estimation, there is good reason to believe no client anxious to purchase the portrait actually exists, and he is only using that to push you."

Diana nodded. "I have thought of that. But I cannot take a chance."

"No. Indeed you cannot."

Diana cleared her throat, anxious to get this last request over with. "However, there is one thing I must ask you to do. Well, actually, *not* to do when you steal the portrait."

"What's that?"

She took a deep breath. "You must promise not to look at it."

6

Hunt stared at her with a blank expression. "Excuse me?"

Diana stood and twisted her fingers. She knew her demand was ridiculous but the thought of Hunt looking at her naked—although from what she'd seen of the portrait, it didn't look *exactly* like her with no clothes since Mr. Mallory had been skimpy on her breasts and hips—had her heart hammering in her chest to the point where she felt as though she would swoon.

"I don't want you to look at it."

"Sit down, Diana. You look like you're about to faint."

She sat, her entire body trembling. "I don't faint."

Hunt joined her on the settee and took her hand in his. "Sweetheart, I cannot steal the portrait without looking at it. How will I know which one to take? Or do you expect me to empty out the gallery in hopes that one of the pictures I steal is yours?"

She chewed her lip and gazed into his deep brown eyes. She'd been looking at those eyes since she was a child, mostly when she needed his help. Yet now they seemed to captivate her as never before. Were they always so soul-searching? Had they always made her feel so tingly inside? She felt as though he could look inside to her very heart.

She raised her chin, ignoring the blush that had risen to her face. "I don't want you to see me. . ."

His full lips quirked in a slight smile, his eyes dancing with mirth. "Yes?"

Diana blew out a deep breath. "You know what I mean."

His mouth broke into a full grin. "Perhaps I do, but to be absolutely sure as to what you are referring, just explain why you do not want me to look at a portrait that I am expected to steal?"

"Very well." Despite her discomfort, she straightened her shoulders and stared into his eyes. "I do not want you to see me naked. There. I said it. Do you understand now?"

He stood and paced, looking back at her, his humor squelched. "So, let me understand this. You want me to go into a studio, under cover of darkness, and steal a portrait that I cannot look at?"

"You make it sound so silly. So impossible."

He placed his hands on his hips and faced her. "It is silly and impossible, Diana. Think about what you're saying. I cannot take a portrait without knowing it's the right one."

She chewed her lip again, knowing full well what he said was correct. But the thought of him looking at her. . .

"Very well. Then this is what I propose." She patted the seat alongside her. She was tired of staring up at him. He was so very tall, and very broad, and very masculine, virile, and she was having a hard time breathing. It must have been that his sizable presence was using up all the air.

Hunt sat and turned to her. "What plan do you have now, sweeting?"

"When you search the portraits, only look at the heads."

Hunt dragged his hand down his face. "All right. I will try—but I can't promise I can do it—to look only at heads and faces."

"Thank you." She smiled and then frowned. "One more thing."

He sighed. "Now what?"

"Once you get it home, you must burn it."

"Burn it?"

"Yes. Burn it."

"Without looking at it, I presume?"

"Of course. You can place it backwards in the fireplace and then burn it." She stared at him for a moment. "What is wrong with your eye?"

"My eye?"

"Yes." She pointed to his face. "You seem to have this tic underneath your right eye."

* * *

ABOUT THREE O'CLOCK THE next morning, not wanting to have his very first genuine thievery—he did not count Miss Manchester's retrieval of her own property as theft—hanging over his head, Hunt dressed all in black and had his butler arrange to have a hackney secured and waiting on the next street. On the off chance someone recognized the crest on his coach, he thought it best to remain as anonymous as possible.

There were still a few carriages returning from events, but the streets were mostly empty. A light mist had begun to fall and that, along with the usual fog, helped to hide anyone traipsing about the area. He had the driver stop a full street from the gallery with instructions to wait for him. From there, he walked, keeping close to the buildings and well into the shadows.

The building housing the gallery stood in the moonless night, a dark shadow amongst others on the street. It was a three-story building and, considering the need for light, he assumed the gallery occupied the top floor.

After a quick glance at the street, Hunt turned and moved deftly alongside the building into the narrow alleyway. His heavy breathing misted in the night air. He squatted in front of the back door and, despite the lack of light, used his sense of touch and considerable skill to open the skimpy lock with a pick; a skill he'd learned as a youth while at Eton. Many a night he and the other lads assuaged their always-present hunger by breaking into the kitchen cupboards.

A slight squeak as he opened the door paused him for a minute. When no sound came from within, he entered and started up the stairs.

That led him to an open room, with no door enclosing it. In the deep shadows, he spotted about twenty paintings displayed on the walls, obviously for sale. He didn't even bother glancing at them since he was certain Mallory would not have the audacity to exhibit Diana's painting. Not if he expected to swindle money from her.

Or live to see the next day.

A quick scan of the room revealed a door that led to a small room. He entered to find six or seven stacks of canvases lining the walls. Much like a large closet, the room had no windows.

He went down on his knees and lit the small lantern he carried with him. He closed the door in case someone was out and about and saw the glow from within and called the Watch. The lantern didn't provide a lot of light, but enough for him to at least see if the paintings were of people, and whether the subject was a man or a woman.

On the third grouping he sorted through, he sucked in a deep breath as the portrait he was looking for sat before him. He pulled it out and rested it at the front of the stack. He let out a low whistle and, leaning back on his heels, he tried—not very hard, admittedly—to look only at Diana's face.

Just to be sure, of course.

He retrieved the lamp from the center of the small room and brought it closer to the painting, only because he needed to make doubly sure it was her, he assured himself.

Despite his best intentions and how much he chastised himself, it wasn't possible to only look at her face. His eyes drifted down. He broke into a sweat, and his mouth dried up. If this painting ever got out, she would be ruined beyond redemption. The only saving grace was that her head was turned in such a way that her hair partially covered her face. It occurred to him that if a person knew Diana quite well, and stared at the picture for a long time, or if she stood right next to it perhaps, only then could she be identified.

But it was not a chance he could take.

Hunt closed his eyes and rubbed them with his thumb and index finger. No matter how hard he tried, he could not get the vision out of his head. He threw the piece of linen he brought with him over the painting and extinguished the lantern.

He walked quickly from the building, down the street to where the hackney awaited him. With a quick nod to the driver, he entered the carriage, placed the covered painting on the seat across from him, leaned his head back, closed his eyes, and took a deep breath.

He'd done it. Diana's reputation had been salvaged. But he had a feeling the torture for him had just begun.

It was a quick ride home and, after paying and dismissing the hackney driver, he made his way around the back of his house and entered through the servants' door. He'd dismissed his valet for the night before he'd left, and with the picture fisted in his hands, he hurried up the stairs to his bedchamber.

A low fire burned in the fireplace, keeping the dampness from the room. Hunt carried the painting to the hearth and set it down with the linen still covering it. He removed his clothes while his conscience fought diligently with his lust.

Sadly, his conscience lost.

Slowly he lifted the linen and gazed at the scandalous portrait in much better light than the studio had provided. Since he knew Diana herself had not posed for it in the nude, he convinced himself he wasn't a voyeur. However, he couldn't help but wonder how accurate Mallory's depiction of her body actually was.

She sat on a solid rose-colored lounge with her arm relaxing on the wooden armrest. Her knees were bent and her legs rested on the seat of the lounge. Her head was tilted down and to the side so her visage wasn't very visible.

Even clothed, the sitting was a bit provocative for a gently-bred young woman. He shook his head. Most likely the influence of her grandmother allowed her to agree to the pose.

Based on her pose, which Diana said Mallory had suggested, Hunt's suspicions grew that the man had planned to duplicate the portrait from the beginning. He apparently had not counted on her leaving the country and held onto the altered version for a year.

He groaned and flipped the linen back down. He stood and paced the room, talking to himself. He was supposed to burn it. He said he would. However, he consoled himself with the fact that he hadn't promised.

But did that truly matter? He sat on the edge of his bed and slumped down, his forearms resting on his thighs, his hands dangling between his spread legs.

He was tired. It was late. He would not decide now.

This was not the best time to burn it anyway. The smell could possibly awaken the entire household.

Since the painting was covered so his valet wouldn't see it in the morning, he turned it to face the wall and would leave it there and make a decision after a few hours of sleep. Despite the painting being burned into his brain, he soon fell into a deep sleep.

With very vivid, very erotic dreams.

About Lady Trouble.

* * *

DIANA PACED HER DRAWING ROOM, wringing her hands and wishing the time would pass faster. Hunt had sent around a note that he would call on her at two o'clock. It was now four minutes to two.

She assumed he had at least gone to Mallory's gallery to retrieve the painting. Wasn't that the reason for him visiting?

Her mind flooded with questions. Suppose the portrait wasn't there? Perhaps he moved it somewhere out of his studio. Or, horrors, maybe he already sold it!

Her heart sped up at the sound of the front door knocker.

She took a deep breath and sat on the settee, her ice-cold hands in her lap as murmurs from Briggs and Hunt reached her ears. Soon footsteps sounded and Diana turned to her chaperone, Mrs. Strickland.

"Will you please go to the kitchen and ask Cook to send tea and leave Lord Huntington and me alone for a few minutes?"

She hurried on when Mrs. Strickland frowned and opened her mouth as if to argue. "You may leave the door open, but there is something we must discuss that is private."

"I don't believe that is proper, my lady."

Diana gritted her teeth. "It is fine. No one will know

we are alone for merely the short time it will take you to retire to the kitchen and request tea. I assure you, I will not get into any trouble."

She swore she heard Mrs. Strickland snort, but ignored it when the woman left just as Hunt entered the room. She really needed to take that woman in hand.

"Well?" She stood, not waiting for the niceties. Her stomach was in knots, and her hands shook.

He stared at her with a strange look on his face. "I recovered the painting."

She let out a deep breath but stopped and looked at him. "But what? You look odd."

"Nothing." He shook his head, and his eyes darted away from her. "All is well." He waved to the settee. "Why don't we sit?"

Something was wrong. Hunt looked at her in a way he'd never looked at her before. She licked her lips. "You didn't. . .I mean, remember I told you not to. . ." Her voice faded.

"Diana, I'm terribly sorry, but there was no way to recover the painting without looking at it. I'm sure that's what you're worried about."

She nodded, a heated flush rising to her face. "Yes, that was a concern."

"Just put it from your mind. Mr. Mallory no longer has the painting. He has no idea where it is, and you are safe."

"But—"

Hunt held up his hand. "I no longer wish to speak about it." With a shaky hand, he tucked an errant curl behind her ear. "It's over."

She grinned with relief and threw herself into Hunt's arms. "Thank you so much."

He pulled her close to his body and groaned.

7

A week passed while Diana was able to breathe and not worry about the portrait. The blasted piece had been retrieved, burned, and she'd heard nothing from Mr. Mallory. That was surprising.

What appeared odd, however, was since then Hunt seemed to be avoiding her.

Normally they would meet at a few social events during the week, but he was absent from each one she'd attended. It was almost like when she was first trying to track him down after her return from Italy. This evening, as she dressed for the Pennington ball, she wondered if he would be present.

She took one last look at herself, pleased with how Marguerite had fixed her hair with a blue ribbon and pearls woven throughout the coiffure. Her pale blue gown, shot through with silver, displaying dark blue embroidery around the neckline, sleeves, and hem, fit her perfectly and made an interesting swishing sound as she walked.

After having Marguerite help her with her necklace and bracelets, Diana attached her earbobs, picked up her reticule and shawl, and left the room. For some reason, she felt more excited about this ball. Perhaps this would be the one that Hunt attended, and she could find out why he appeared to be avoiding her.

Hunt.

In the time she'd spent in Italy he had rarely crossed her mind. In fact, it wasn't until she needed his help with the portrait that she thought of him after her return. Odd that, since they'd been friends since childhood.

Now, however, she couldn't get him out of her mind. His crooked smile, the scent of bay rum that wafted from him, his broad shoulders, emphasized by the fine cut of his clothing, and his a-bit-too-long hair that curled over his cravat. Had he always been so tempting?

Surely he had been, since she'd noted the looks he received from young and old women alike upon entering a ballroom, but she'd always been indifferent to him, thinking of Hunt as a brother.

That was no longer true. The thoughts that had been running through her head were anything but brotherlike.

"Are you ready, Mrs. Strickland?" Diana turned so Briggs could help her with her shawl. It matched her gown but was lined with satin, making it warm enough for the night air.

Her chaperone made her way from the back of the house, pulling on her gloves. "Yes. I am ready to leave, my lady."

The two women descended the steps and entered Diana's carriage. The vehicle had belonged to her grandmama and still bore the Abbott crest, but Diana did not have the heart to replace the carriage, even though it was more than twenty years old.

Since there had been no living direct heir when Grandfather passed, the obscure family member who had inherited the title lived a solitary life in an estate near the Scottish border. He had hired a steward and household staff enough to maintain the property. As far as Diana knew, he'd never even visited the place.

The inside of her carriage held the faint scent of Grandmama, although Diana feared she was fooling herself, and it was merely part imagination and part stubbornness to admit Grandmama was truly gone.

Their arrival was swift, but after waiting in a carriage line for about fifteen minutes, they finally reached the Pennington townhouse. A footman opened the door and helped them out. They made their way up the steps, surrendered their shawls, and proceeded up to the first floor ballroom, handing the invitation to the footman announcing the attendees.

"Lady Diana Pemberton."

As she and Mrs. Strickland descended the stairs, Diana's eyes immediately scanned the room, her heart speeding up when she noticed Hunt standing with two other gentlemen. Hunt held a glass of some sort of beverage in his hand and leaned one shoulder against the wall as they conversed.

His head whipped around when her name was announced. He straightened and handed his glass to a passing footman. He continued to study her as she reached the floor and was immediately surrounded by her friends.

Over Miss Spencer-Roth's shoulder, Diana watched Hunt make his way across the ballroom, stopping to chat here and there, but his eyes always returning to her. She shivered. The look in his eyes was disconcerting.

Lady St. John stepped in front of him, leaning a little too close, then placing her hand on his chest in a very forward move. He smiled at her, and Diana immediately grew annoyed. The woman was a known flirt. Not only flirting but inviting various men to her bed while her husband occupied himself in his mistress's bed.

Diana told herself it was truly no business of hers if Hunt availed himself of her offer.

Then why was she so irritated as she watched their exchange?

Hunt stepped back a bit but then took the small dance card dangling from her wrist that she waved in his face and wrote his name. Lady St. John looked at the card and frowned, but he merely offered a slight bow and continued to move in Diana's direction.

"Lady Diana, don't you agree?" Lord Astley's question drew Diana's attention from Hunt.

"I'm sorry, my lord, but I'm afraid I was woolgathering."

Astley stiffened. Full of self-importance, he apparently did not like the idea that his comments were not attended to. He sighed as if attempting to get through to a slow child. "I asked if you believed that the Devon musicale next Thursday would be a trying event to sit through." He grinned and looked around the circle, most of them nodding and smiling along with him.

Miss Devon and her sister, Miss Amelia Devon, were forced by their overbearing mother to perform at least once a year. The young ladies were sweet girls with very little talent. Diana hated to think this group would laugh and snicker at the poor girls who were being bullied into doing something they did not want to do.

But then Lord Astley was a known gossiper and nasty in his comments about almost everyone.

"I don't believe so, my lord. I always look forward to the event." She caught Hunt's eye as he moved closer. Diana gave a slight curtsey to no one in particular. "If you will excuse me, I see my chaperone is summoning me."

Luckily, none in the group turned to see where Diana headed since no one would believe for one minute that Lord Huntington, with his rakish reputation, was acting as her chaperone.

Her heart thudded, and her mouth dried up as she reached him. This was complete silliness. She'd known Hunt forever. For goodness sake he taught her to swim wearing only her chemise. Of course she had been only eight years at the time and he twelve.

Hunt bowed. "Good evening, my lady."

She dipped. "Good evening to you, my lord."

He extended his arm. "Let's take a stroll."

So this is what they'd come to? Formal greetings and a stroll around the ballroom? 'Twas almost as if they were strangers.

* * *

HUNT GRIMACED AT THEIR EXCHANGE. 'Twas almost as if they were strangers. He drew Diana closer as they made their way through the throng to the edge of the ballroom where there was a bit of space for them to walk.

He'd tried to avoid her since he'd told Diana about the portrait's recovery. Why? He wasn't absolutely clear. He'd known the woman all his life. He'd rescued her from so many mishaps he'd lost count. But there was something about this last entanglement that had him on edge in her presence.

Maybe the fact that I saw a painting of her naked and, despite her request that I burn it, it still sits in the wardrobe in the bedchamber next to mine.

The past week he'd spent time at his clubs and at The Rose Room, telling himself he was there to make sure business was running as it should. Only after Dante and Driscoll both ordered him from the place since he was disrupting their routine did he admit he was evading the normal social events he would generally attend to avoid Diana.

"I haven't seen you all week, my lord."

Hunt shook his head and smiled at her. "Diana, let's stop the 'my lord' 'my lady' business. I think we feel uncomfortable with each other because of the painting. Let's put it aside and go back to the way we were."

"And what way was that, Hunt? I've been gone for a year. The first time I saw you after my return, I asked you to retrieve a scandalous portrait for me."

"Friends, Diana. We've always been friends." He almost believed it himself. Yes, they had always been friends, but he could never be friends again with the woman in the portrait. He was simply too full of lust when he was near her.

So where did that leave them?

"Are you going to the Grafton house party this weekend?" Diana asked, not looking him in the eye. She was acting as strange as he felt.

He shook his head. "I don't plan on it. I will be quite busy with straightening out some of my investments." Bloody hell, couldn't he come up with a better excuse than that? He had no intention of straightening business matters or going to the blasted house party. The idea of him and Diana under the same roof. All night. Only rooms away...

He shuddered at the temptation. He had never bedded a virgin and had no intention of starting with Diana. Unless they were betrothed. However, as fond as he was of her, Diana did jump from one disaster to another. As her husband, some poor man—not him—would spend all his time defending her honor and dodging scandal.

Hunt could never be that husband. Between his work with the Crown and his need to keep his title shame-free, his newly-discovered lust for Diana would end nowhere. Despite her reputation for trouble, she was still a gently-bred young lady of the *ton* and hands off for any gentleman not looking to step into the parson's noose.

He had no need for the temptation of a house party.

"Oh, that's too bad. I hear it will be quite fun and Lady Grafton and her daughter Lady Eunice have a number of activities planned. I think Lord Grafton intends to have a shooting contest, as well."

None of that would tempt Hunt as much as Diana would every minute of every day during the house party. "I am sorry, my dear, but I don't think I will make it."

She shrugged, but he saw definite disappointment on her face.

"There you are!" Lady St. John walked up to them and tapped Hunt on his arm. "It is almost time for our dance."

He sighed inwardly. The last thing he wanted to do was spend the next twenty or so minutes dodging Lady St. John's wandering hands. At least, due to his diligence, the dance coming up was a cotillion and not a waltz.

Before he walked off with Lady St. John, he reached for Diana's dance card. The supper waltz was open. Had she saved it for him? Hoping they would meet at this event? He quickly scribbled his name next to the number and offered her a slight bow.

He glanced back at her as he led Lady St. John to the dance floor. Diana was staring at the dance card with a slight smile on her face.

THE NEXT MORNING, Hunt entered the breakfast room still out of sorts after the night before. The waltz with Diana had been torturous. He wanted to pull her against him and feel the curves he'd witnessed in the portrait. She'd felt so very right in his arms. They even grinned at each other like a couple of love-sick fools.

Hopefully, no one noticed. The last thing he needed were rumors.

After taking his seat, he snapped open the freshly-ironed newspaper sitting next to his plate and folded it to the front page. He reached for his cup of tea, and his hand stopped halfway there. He blinked several times to make sure his eyesight hadn't failed him. There was no mistake. The morning newspaper headline remained the same.

Mallory Art Gallery burned to the ground

Owner, J. D. Mallory dead

Before he even had the chance to read the story, one of his footmen entered with an envelope resting on a salver. "This just came for you, my lord."

Hunt took the envelope, broke the seal, and opened it. From the Home Office.

My Lord,

Your presence is requested this morning at ten o'clock.

Sir Phillip DuBois-Gifford

8

Sir Phillip DuBois-Gifford received a salary from the Home Office and bore the title Covert Agent, but to Hunt's knowledge, no record of his employment existed anywhere. He worked on difficult cases that the Crown felt were far too delicate or sensitive to be handled through normal channels. It was generally Sir Phillip who summoned one of the Rose brothers for help.

Hunt entered the modest, indistinct house in a lower-class neighborhood that served as Sir Phillip's office. The man himself was nondescript in his bearing, looks, and manner of clothing. No one seeing Sir Phillip on the street would take him for more than a typical resident of the area. A lower income worker.

Hunt was convinced DuBois-Gifford lived a totally different life elsewhere in London. Since he was so unnoticeable, there was a good chance Hunt had seen him when out and about and never recognized him. He'd learned from the beginning of their relationship to keep his questions to himself.

Sir Phillip stood and shook Hunt's hand as he entered the small, stuffy office in the house. "Thank you for coming, my lord. Please have a seat."

Hunt sat and rested his booted foot on his knee. "How can I be of service, Sir Phillip?" Even though they'd worked together on more than a few projects, they'd never gotten past the formality of the aristocrat and the commoner.

"Are you familiar with the J. D. Art Gallery?"

Hunt sat up, his heart taking an extra thump. "Yes." No point in offering more than necessary.

"It burned down last night."

Hunt nodded, still cautious. "I read that."

DuBois-Gifford picked up a paper weight sitting on his desk and rubbed his thumb over it. "Mr. Mallory's body was found in the burned-out building. However, he did not die from burns or smoke inhalation. He'd been shot twice at close range."

Hunt did a good job of hiding his surprise. "It is believed to be a murder?"

"Yes. The fire had been set after the man was shot. We cannot assess if anything was taken from the building, but since his gallery was full of paintings, we have no way of knowing if something was removed before the murder. Our people are attempting to find invoices or contracts, but a lot of that information was burned."

He breathed easier knowing there wouldn't be a contract or invoice on Diana's portrait.

"In fact, as we are certain he was murdered, that is where you come in."

Hunt waited for the man to continue, his thoughts running wild about the information he just received. Perhaps Diana was not the only person Mallory was blackmailing.

His ideas were quickly quashed when Sir Phillip continued. "We have reason to believe that Mr. Mallory was working with a group of men who are anarchists with the intention of bringing down the British government."

Hunt let out a low whistle. "Interesting."

"Indeed." DuBois-Gifford leaned forward. "Supposedly Mallory was about to leave the country with information damaging to the group. Even more interesting is a man who is working—and possibly leading—the group is a member of parliament."

"An MP is working to take down the government?" Hunt's eyebrows shot up. "Who?"

"Actually he is a member of the House of Lords."

"A peer," he breathed. Hunt shook his head, not shocked, but certainly surprised at Sir Phillip's revelation.

"We don't have a name yet, but our contacts have told us that this gentleman is indeed active in Society and will be attending a house party this coming weekend at Lord and Lady Grafton's estate in Essex."

Oh, no.

A sense of foreboding came over him. "And?"

"And we want you to gather as much information as you can by attending this party. Our target will be meeting a contact there who we are told is one of the staff. If you can pick up information on who this lord is, we can crush this entire group before they cause irreparable damage."

Hunt stared out the window, taking in all Sir Phillip told him.

"I assume you have been sent an invitation since we know you are welcomed at all these things," DuBois-Gifford waved his hand. Perhaps with disdain at the frivolous lifestyle of the Upper Crust who have time for such nonsense as house parties.

"Yes. As a matter of fact, I was invited but intended to decline."

"Not anymore."

The Crown had spoken.

. . .

HUNT CONSIDERED his newest assignment as he returned home. It was difficult to accept that a member of the House of Lords would be involved in an attempt to overthrow the government. It went against everything the Crown stood for and a titled peer had every reason to see that the status quo stood. What benefit could he possibly gain?

On the other hand, he would now be under the same roof as Diana for the length of the house party. Something he had planned to avoid at all costs. If he remembered correctly, the guests were expected to arrive on Friday afternoon and spend five days visiting, playing games, dancing, shooting, all the things popular for any house party.

That meant four nights with Diana merely down the corridor from him. In her nightgown. In her bed, all warm and soft. With all that luxurious hair hanging down, most likely in a soft plait as most women were apt to do when they slept.

He groaned. It would be a long five days.

And nights.

* * *

DIANA, Mrs. Strickland, and Marguerite stepped from the carriage with the assistance of a footman at Lord and Lady Grafton's estate in the county of Essex. Most of the other ladies would have sent their lady's maids ahead in another carriage to supervise the unloading and setting up of their mistress's wardrobe in their assigned room, but Diana didn't see the need to do that.

Plus, since she was alone, it made for a more pleasant ride to be able to converse with the two women. Most of the Upper Crust did not chat with the help; something that Diana had never ascribed to.

As much as she'd been looking forward to this break from the Season events, especially with her portrait problem solved, she felt a tad disappointed that Hunt wouldn't be joining the group. It amazed her that someone who she'd been friends with for years all of a sudden appeared so different to her, and whose presence she craved.

His actual visage had not changed—although since her return he did seem larger and more commanding—but the change was in how her body reacted to his nearness. Parts of her body she had never paid much attention to seemed to come alive when she regarded him across a ballroom or was held in his arms as they waltzed. Especially when he flashed that rakish smile that had many women attempting to lure him into their beds.

Even though she acknowledged her confusing and strong attraction to him since her return from Italy, there was no reason to believe anything would ever come of it.

She'd known for years that the Earl of Huntington viewed her as a walking disaster. She was also aware from their years of friendship that, when it came time to marry, he would choose a young debutante who was pure, biddable, and had nary a misstep attached to her name.

She sighed. She was so far from that image as to be farcical. If only she were as bold as Grandmama and suggested to Hunt that they have an affair. Despite what most members of the *ton* thought of her, however, she longed for what every other young lady wanted. A husband who cared for her, a home she could manage, and children to love and raise.

"Good afternoon, Lady Diana, I am so pleased you were able to join us." Lady Grafton greeted her, kissing the air on either side of her face.

"Thank you, my lady, I am happy to be here."

Lady Eunice joined her mother, squealing in that very annoying way the poor girl oftentimes did. Eunice was getting close to spinsterhood, which was a pity because, underneath her silly demeanor, she was a lovely young lady who would make some man a fine wife. Except Diana had noticed a bit of desperation in the girl this current Season.

Eunice would have already been settled in her own home with a husband and children but for her parents' insistence she marry the highest title she could.

Eunice linked her arm with Diana's and led her toward the house. "We are going to have so much fun. I have a few games in mind that will probably cause some raised eyebrows." She giggled again.

"Indeed?"

"Yes. And Mother just told me yesterday that the Earl of Huntington will be joining us. I am so excited about that because he took so long to respond, Mother was sure he would decline." They maneuvered their way past Lady Grafton and a couple she was greeting, then entered the hall and started up the stairs.

Hunt? He told her he was not able to join the festivities. Diana attempted to tamp down her growing excitement at Eunice's words, else she begin to giggle like her hostess.

"I am pleased to hear that," Diana said, hoping she sounded as blasé as she wanted to appear.

"I know. I hate to admit it, but I am quite enamored with the earl, and so are my parents." Eunice leaned in close as if to offer a major secret. "He asked me to dance at the Marlowe ball." She closed her eyes and dipped as if dancing. "It was wonderful."

Diana grabbed the girl's arm before she waltzed down the stairs backward. "Careful."

Another giggle.

Eunice left Diana at the room she'd been assigned. Marguerite was already unpacking and Mrs. Strickland supervising, which obviously annoyed Marguerite. "Mrs. Strickland, I understand there are two rooms on the top floor set aside for companions since this room is rather small. Perhaps you can get yourself set up there," Diana said.

Marguerite mouthed "thank you" as Mrs. Strickland nodded and picked up her travel bag. "Very well. I will see you at dinner, I suppose. Unless the companions are to be banned to another area for dinner as well." She sniffed and left the room.

Diana rolled her eyes and ignored the comment. Mrs. Strickland could be a trial at times, but Diana didn't have the desire or time to interview another companion. She would be quite happy to do without one, but since she always seemed to be in danger of getting into trouble, having a companion who acted as chaperone was a necessity to keep the *virtue vultures* happy.

"Marguerite, they are serving tea on the patio. I would love to be rid of this dusty outfit. Will you see if there is something that doesn't require pressing that I may change into?"

"Yes, my lady. Why don't you wash up at the water bowl one of the maids just filled and I will find something for you." The maid nodded at the milk glass bowl and pitcher on the dresser across from the bed.

Diana washed and with Marguerite's help changed into a deep yellow *mousselaine de soie* gown that drew snug across her stomach and midriff with a lovely gathering at her lower back, not like the horsehair bustles of the past, but small ruffles and one large bow.

Diana loved that dress because her full-figured, muscular form from all her riding filled out her outfits quite well. Since she never wanted to be like everyone else, she relished in her body, different from the current waifs.

. . .

SHE WAS DIRECTED to the patio by one of the footmen. It was a pleasant day, with some sunshine, but combined with enough passing clouds to not require a parasol to protect her skin. She noticed most of the young ladies present did carry one with them. Diana always hated carrying reticules, parasols and other hinderances to free movement.

"Diana!" Miss April Connors called to her from a small table where she sat with her brother, Mr. Nelson Connors and their mother, Mrs. Edith Connors. Mr. Ernest Connors, the patriarch, was missing.

Diana made her way to the table, her insides twisting at the leering stare coming from the younger Mr. Connor's eyes. They traveled up and down her body as if assessing a bit of horseflesh at Tattersalls. Apparently, her absence from England hadn't been long enough for some young men to forget her stumble into disgrace. She'd never cared for any of the Connors, anyway.

Mr. Ernest Connors was a blustering, large man who used every opportunity to remind one and all that despite being a 'mister' he was the son of a viscount and only one step from inheriting, since his brother, the current viscount, had been married for several years and had still not produced an heir.

His wife was timid and meek, a trait Diana barely tolerated in a woman. Nelson had always regarded Diana with a combination of disdain and ungentlemanly interest and poor April had been betrothed to a young man who left for the continent on a trip and, after four years, had still not returned, leaving the girl a bit on the sour side.

Mr. Connors rose and pulled out a chair. "My lady, if you please."

Diana took the seat across from Miss Connors and, unfortunately, next to Mr. Connors, who inched his chair ever so slightly so he was closer to her than she would have liked.

After his knee touched her thigh, she wished she had brought a parasol after all. She could stick him in the leg with it.

"I'm so glad to see you, Lady Diana. I hadn't heard that you returned from your visit with your family in Italy." Miss Connors offered a warm smile while her brother gave a low, but noticeable snort.

"Yes, I had a lovely time." She nodded. "And I am glad to see all of you as well."

A footman arrived at the table with a pot of tea and a tray of several small sandwiches, tarts, and biscuits.

The group made typical inane conversation about the roads and the weather while everyone fixed their tea and placed various offerings on their plate. Diana took a sip and, instantly, the hairs on the back of her neck rose.

He's here.

9

Against his better judgment, but at the request of Sir Phillip DuBois-Gifford, Hunt had returned home from the meeting with Sir Phillip and immediately sent an acceptance missive to Lady Grafton. He managed to avoid Diana for the next few days by spending more time at his club and less at typical *ton* affairs.

It hadn't helped one bit. He still dreamed of her and, whenever his mind was not fully occupied, his thoughts drifted to Diana and the portrait still sitting in the wardrobe. He really ought to burn it, but every time he seriously considered doing so, he found one reason or another to not.

Now he stood on the patio at the Grafton Estate staring at Diana's back as she sat with the Connors family.

"My lord, I am so glad you have arrived!" Lady Eunice grabbed his arm, taking him by surprise, almost pitching him to the ground.

"My lady, how nice to see you." He glanced in the direction of the Connors' table. Diana turned and smirked at him. Either because he had said he was not attending or, most likely, at the circumstances he found himself in with his hostess.

"Please join me for tea, my lord. I have a lovely table over here." Lady Eunice practically dragged him across the patio to a table for two set alongside the balustrade lining the patio. Off into a corner away from the others.

It appeared she had been waiting for him since it was already set with two places and a tray of sweets. Once they were seated, a footman appeared with a pot of tea.

"How do you like your tea, my lord?" She batted her eyelashes at him as she poured. He was concerned that she would spill the hot liquid if she didn't pay attention to what she was doing.

"A bit of sugar and some cream." He glanced across the patio at Diana, and his stomach muscles tightened at the look Nelson Connors was casting in her direction. He was leaning closer to her, and Diana was tilting away. The rake had better keep his hands where Hunt could see them.

"My lord, I have planned so many games for the party. I hope you enjoy charades,"—he hated it—"blindman's buff,"—hated that one also—"and forfeits"—the one he hated most of all. She grinned with a look in her eye he'd seen from many a hopeful debutante over the years.

He groaned inwardly. It appeared reining in his lust with thoughts of a soft and sensual Diana in a warm bed in the same house, on the same floor, with only two wooden doors separating them would not be his only problem.

Since he'd been forced to attend this gathering, his intention had been to get the information Sir Phillip required as quickly as possible, plead a problem that needed his attention in London to his hosts, and then leave early.

When he'd planned his early escape, it had been for

the sole purpose of avoiding the temptation Diana presented, but now it appeared he would be dodging Lady Eunice most of the time as well. That situation could be even more of a problem if the young lady hung about him the entire time, making it difficult to conduct his investigation.

The best solution was to stick close to Diana, which was precisely what he did not want to do. At least with all the secrets he and Diana had shared over the years, he could employ her help.

With her guile she could provide assistance. She was a great talker and could wile anyone into revealing information. Yes, he would have to divulge the reason for his attendance at the party.

He realized that all the time he'd been thinking about Diana and the investigation, Lady Eunice had been blathering on and on. He'd nodded a few times and hoped like hell he hadn't agreed to anything foolish or time-consuming. The last time he had drifted off when a young lady had spoken with him, he found he'd promised to escort her to the museum the next day. Along with her doting parents casting warm and very frightening—for him—glances in their direction.

"If you will excuse me, my lady, I have a message to deliver to Lady Diana." He placed his napkin on the table and stood. As crass as that sounded, he had to get away from Lady Eunice before he said or did something ungentlemanly.

He knew when he asked her to dance at the Marlowe ball it had been a mistake. She apparently had read more into it than she should have.

At first he'd thought Lady Eunice might be someone he could consider to court, but after only a few minutes into the dance, he'd decided he would rather pass his title onto his brother than marry Lady Eunice or anyone of her ilk. Although she'd appeared sweet, it became apparent her interest lay in money, titles and status.

His attempts thus far to find a woman to court had been for nil. Every young lady he'd considered turned out to be someone he could barely tolerate throughout a dance or dinner, never mind for the rest of his life.

When considering a wife, it would help if he didn't find it a chore to bed her but, aside from that, his main concerns were someone who would not tarnish his title, who would conduct herself properly in all circumstances, run an efficient household, and raise well-behaved children.

"Oh." Lady Eunice looked at him with surprise, then smiled. "Of course, we have plenty of time to spend together, and I must see to some matters about dinner, anyway."

He bowed and hurried away.

Of course, we have plenty of time to spend together.

What the devil did that mean? Now he was really concerned.

He approached Lady Diana just as she was mumbling something to Nelson Connors which did not look like an invitation. In fact, she looked as though she was ready to flatten him. Knowing Diana as he did, he wouldn't take wagers that she'd not do that very thing.

"Lady Diana. May I have a word with you please?" He bowed briefly at the other three. "Mrs. Connors, Miss Connors." He glared at Nelson. "Connors."

Nelson returned his glare with raised eyebrows. As if he had no idea why Hunt looked as though he wanted to haul him up and pummel him.

Diana stood when he pulled back her chair. "It's been lovely speaking with all of you. I hope you enjoy the party."

She turned and took his extended arm, and they moved away from the table. Hunt maneuvered them past a few other tables, down the stone steps to the garden below.

"What did Nelson say to you?" Hunt's voice must have come out stronger than he intended because Diana looked up at him, wide-eyed.

She waved her hand and faced forward. "Nothing to concern yourself with. He's an annoying man."

"But what did he say?"

"Does it really matter?"

Hunt gritted his teeth. "Yes. It does."

Diana huffed. "He suggested I might be open to a dalliance with him while we're here."

"I'll kill him." Hunt turned to head back to the patio when Diana grabbed his arm.

"No. Just let it go. I made certain he knew not only would I never consider such a thing with him—or anyone—if he ever spoke to me again in that manner I would injure him in an area that would leave him unable to 'dally' with anyone for a while."

Hunt burst out laughing. Leave it to Diana to come straight to the point. He still didn't like the idea that Connors thought Diana would even consider such a thing.

Diana grinned back at him. "He turned quite pale, actually. I don't think I will be troubled with him again."

That might be so, but Hunt planned to have a little chat with Connors to make sure he knew that, not only would Diana keep him from 'dallying,' Hunt would follow it up with a beating that would keep him in bed for days.

Their stroll took them past a grouping of bluebells and cowslip. "I thought you said you were unable to attend the house party?" Diana asked.

He walked them over to a stone bench under a dogwood tree. Once they settled, he said, "Can a man not change his mind? Or is that only a woman's prerogative?"

"No. A man can change his mind, but I've not known you to vacillate. Once you make up your mind, you rarely change it."

Again he toyed with the idea of bringing Diana into his confidence. She could keep Lady Eunice at bay so he could conduct his investigation. However, this was a sensitive matter and, although he had no reason to believe Diana would compromise his assignment, he would still be breeching protocol. Maybe if he told her only enough to get her cooperation without revealing the entire matter, it would assuage his conscience.

Hunt cleared his throat. "Actually, Diana, you are correct. I don't usually change my mind. However, I am here for a specific purpose. To gather information for someone at the Home Office."

Her eyes grew wide. "*The* Home Office?"

"Yes. Once in a while they ask my assistance on something that is very sensitive when they don't want to go through the regular channels."

Diana's mouth dropped. "You're a spy?"

"Shh." Hunt looked around. "Hardly. But in this case, I need to be able to move freely and observe various people. Lady Eunice hinted—no, she flat out stated—that she intended to spend a lot of time with me."

Diana's eyes snapped. "The hussy!"

Hunt grinned.

* * *

DIANA WAS NOT ONLY surprised by Hunt's revelation about the Home Office but impressed. She'd known Hunt all her life and never had she suspected that he did work for the department.

"I can help."

Hunt blanched. "No. I only want you to keep Lady Eunice away so I can do what I need to do."

"Well maybe not really help, but I could cause a distraction now and then so you can sneak off."

Hunt closed his eyes. "Diana, I tremble to think of what sort of a distraction you could cause." Despite his words, he turned toward her and offered a smile.

They stood and continued their walk, and Diana became uncomfortably aware of how her body was reacting to this innocuous stroll. She'd been telling herself for days there was no attraction between the two of them, that it was all her imagination.

No. She'd been fooling herself. Something had shifted between them and, not only was she feeling it, but it was quite possible Hunt did as well. She decided to take the bull by the horn.

"Have you been avoiding me?"

She felt Hunt's muscles tense under her arm.

"No. Why would you say that?"

"Well, perhaps because for the past week I didn't see you at any of the normal events a man who is looking for a bride would attend."

He glanced down at her. "Who said I was looking for a bride?"

"You did." She tilted her head to look into his eyes. "And I heard it from a number of people after I returned from Italy. Apparently when one of the most eligible bachelors in the *ton* makes it known he is ready to settle down and set up his nursery, ferocious mamas and desperate daughters take note."

He shrugged. "It had crossed my mind. I am not getting any younger."

Why did that bother her so much? The thought of Hunt marrying and taking a sweet, silly debutante to his bed and into his life depressed her. Someone perfect, of course. Not like her with her scandals and other mishaps.

A blasé attitude would be best. "Any prospects?"

Just when she decided he wasn't going to answer, he said, "No. Not really." He kept his face forward and didn't look at her.

That was not a sense of relief she felt. No. It didn't matter to her one whit if he had his eyes set on someone or not.

It didn't matter at all.

10

Three days of the blasted house party had passed, and Hunt was no closer to obtaining the name of the person working to bring down the government than upon arrival.

Despite Diana's best attempts to keep Lady Eunice away from him, the young girl found more reasons for him to assist her than one could imagine. It got to the point where he almost asked her if she employed any footmen.

The games had been as silly and degrading as he'd feared, but Diana had come through once or twice by asking him to walk with her in the garden to get a breath of fresh air.

Although it would leave them open to speculation, they didn't return to the drawing room until the tea carts had rolled out. There were a few raised eyebrows, but since Hunt and Diana had been in view of other couples the entire time, nothing was said.

Except Lady Eunice had looked daggers at Diana.

Today, Lady Grafton had set up a trip to town for the guests. They would visit Roman ruins outside the town, then do some shopping and meet afterwards at a local pub for lunch.

Hunt stepped out of the front door and immediately went to Diana's side. "Do not leave me alone today," he murmured from the side of his mouth.

Diana laughed, a hardy sound that one would never hear from any other young lady of the *ton*. She leaned closer and whispered. "Are you afraid of someone, my lord? Do you need protection from pirates or other brigands?"

"Not funny. I don't expect to uncover any information in a trip to town, but Lady Eunice and Miss Allison have taken turns talking my ear off, and I prefer a morning of peace and quiet."

"And you think to get peace and quiet from me?" Diana laughed even harder.

"Your type of peace and quiet I've been handling for years, my sweet."

Diana took the arm he offered. "Were I you, I would be more concerned with one of them attempting to make it appear as if you compromised her."

"Yes, there is that, too."

He couldn't help but think of Diana's flight to Italy after the same thing happened to her. Except she hadn't been the one who'd planned the discovery of them together. It had been Viscount Stratford, eager to get his hands on Diana's money. She'd been wise to refuse to marry him. The man would have made her life miserable.

But she paid the price.

There were only two days left to gather information before they returned to London. So far he'd not seen any of the staff speaking with a guest, except for the normal interaction one would see at any house party.

He'd taken to wandering the halls at night to see if anyone had left their room to consult with a staff member. All he'd gotten for his trouble was frustration at the arousing sounds coming from behind the doors.

House parties were notorious for bed partner switching.

Prowling the corridor, all he could think of was Diana in her bed, soft and warm and dressed only in a nightgown. And under that nightgown were curves he'd seen, even if they were not completely accurate. He had to stop torturing himself.

He would be happy when this blasted party was over.

THE NEXT MORNING, Hunt helped Diana into one of the carriages, and they were immediately joined by Lady Eunice and Miss Allison.

He offered a slight bow. "Good morning, ladies. It looks like a perfectly pleasant day for a trip into town." Hunt smiled at the two girls, hoping they did not plan to tag along with him and Diana.

"Yes. This is delightful weather," Miss Allison agreed.

There were several carriages transporting the guests to town. All those who planned to enjoy the outing had arranged themselves in the various vehicles. Diana's companion, Mrs. Strickland, had apparently decided not to join the group, which was fine with Hunt. He didn't really care for the woman, and he hoped to have some time alone with Diana.

"Say, I hope you don't mind if I join the group," Nelson Connors said as he climbed into the carriage and sat next to Diana. With the two young ladies across from them, it would have made more sense for him to sit there, instead of crowding him and Diana.

Hunt's jaw tensed as Diana shifted a bit, so she and Connors were not touching. She'd already made it perfectly clear to the man that she was not interested in him or the idea of a dalliance, so what was his game?

At least it wasn't a long ride into town, so Hunt

concentrated instead on the lack of progress in the investigation. He didn't like to fail and the prospect of returning with no name frustrated him.

* * *

THE CARRIAGES BEGAN to roll away from the manor in a line. "Where are you off to this morning?" Diana asked the two young ladies across from them.

Both girls looked in Hunt's direction. He looked out the window.

"I don't know, actually. There is just so much to see. . ." Miss Allison continued to gape at Hunt who maintained his interest in the scenery.

Lady Eunice had no qualms in getting what she wanted. "Where are you headed, my lord?"

Hunt faced her but, before he could answer, Diana said, "Oh, his lordship has promised to accompany me to the bookstore. I understand it is a wonderful one for a small town."

"Yes, that is what I hear," Lady Eunice mumbled.

"I'm sure you've been there many times. It would be boring for you," Diana said.

Lady Eunice narrowed her eyes at what she must have considered a sabotage from Diana. "Actually, I have never been there."

"I agree, bookstores are boring," Mr. Connors said. "I suggest you two ladies join me in a walk to the Roman ruins. That is much more interesting."

Diana was thrilled. She wanted some time alone with Hunt, and Mr. Connors had just provided the perfect excuse. "Yes, do go with Mr. Connors to the ruins. I've already seen them, and I believe you will be as fascinated as I was. I'm sure Lord Huntington and I will be in the bookstore for some time."

Apparently, Mr. Connors now had his eye on one of the young ladies. It was known that he had a problem with drink and gambling, which was why he most likely needed a wife with deep pockets to continue his lifestyle. As far as Diana knew, both Miss Allison and Lady Eunice came with nice dowries.

As they continued the ride, Diana had a hard time not noticing Hunt's closeness. She had automatically shifted toward him when Mr. Connors entered the carriage and sat next to her. It was a good idea at the time, but now she was trapped next to Hunt, captured by the heat coming from his body and the enticing scent from his bath soap.

She really needed to stop this nonsense. If there was any woman in all of London who would be the least appropriate bride for the Earl of Huntington, it was her. Over the years, she'd learned what Hunt wanted in a wife, and one of the simpering young ladies sitting across from them was perfect.

Then why was he dodging them? And asking her to 'protect' him from Lady Eunice's wiles? Were they not prime examples of a 'perfect' Lady Huntington?

She snuck a side glance at Hunt who still stared out the window. Mr. Connors had the girls involved in a conversation about the various events of the Season so far and what was to come.

Diana was more interested in Hunt. Did he truly want a wife who was so placid and mellow? As well as she knew the man, she didn't believe he would be happy with that sort of a wife. But wherever her thoughts led her, one thing was certain. He would never want her. And, in some ways, that hurt.

Once they arrived at the town center, Mr. Connors held both elbows out to the ladies, and off they went. Neither one of the girls looked happy.

"That was easy," Diana said as she took Hunt's arm.

"For as annoyed as I was when Connors climbed into our carriage, I am now grateful to him."

The bookstore was a mere few steps from where the

carriages left the guests. Diana was already impressed before they opened the door. Despite it being a small town, the place was quite large and took up a goodly space on the square. The large window in the front held a display of books relevant to the season.

A soft tinkle from a bell at the top of the door announced their arrival. Several people browsed the shelves, and a young mother sat on a comfortable chair next to the wall with a small child on her lap, reading him a story.

"This is a lovely bookstore!" Diana said as she turned in a circle to view all the shelves of books.

"I'm glad you think so. Welcome to Brenner's Book Store." An older man, a bit stooped over with a scant number of strands of white hair on his head and thick spectacles perched on his nose approached them. Despite his age, he was cheerful, with rosy cheeks and bright, twinkling blue eyes. He was the sort of man one liked immediately.

"Good morning, my lord, my lady. I hope you find something interesting and enlightening here in my humble bookstore."

"Oh, I'm sure we will. Are you Mr. Brenner?"

"Yes, indeed. Although I am not the original Mr. Brenner. That was my grandfather, and then my father."

"Ah. Keeping the business in the family, I see," Hunt said.

Mr. Brenner nodded. "Please take your time and browse to your heart's content."

Hunt went in the direction of the shelves that were marked as Land Management and Diana was almost—but not quite—embarrassed to make her way to the fiction bookshelves.

Mr. Brenner had a good selection of fiction, so Diana intended to be engaged for quite a while.

After about twenty minutes, her attention was taken

up by two men on the other side of the shelf from where she stood. They were speaking in a low voice, and one of the voices sounded familiar.

Keeping an open book in her hand, she walked slowly to where Hunt was, taking a quick glance at the two men as she passed. One was very tall and broad and, even though she could not see his face, she was quite certain he was one of the footmen at the Grafton estate.

His large body blocked the man he was speaking with. She continued to where Hunt was just sliding a book back onto the shelf.

He turned to her and smiled. He must have seen something in her eyes because he frowned. "What?"

She leaned forward, and he dipped his head so he could hear her. "There are two men on the other side of the fiction bookshelves. I am quite certain one of them is a footman from Grafton's. He's blocking the other man so I can't see him, but his voice sounds familiar."

Hunt nodded to the three books she held in her arms. "Are you purchasing those?"

"Yes."

He took her by the elbow and walked her to the front of the store. Mr. Brenner was at the front desk. "Well, it looks like you found something to your liking, my lady."

"Yes. I did. I would like these three books. I am so looking forward to reading them."

Mr. Brenner added up the cost, and Diana dug in her reticule and retrieved the coins to pay him.

He smiled at her as he handed her the change. "You have a wonderful day."

Hunt and Diana thanked the man and left the store. "Now what?" she said.

"We wait in a place where we cannot be seen. Soon one or both men will exit the store." He walked her over to a park bench on the green, across from the bookstore.

They chatted amiably while a few people went in and out of the store. After about five minutes the footman left the store, looked around, and walked off. No more than two minutes later, one of the guests at the house party left and walked toward the pub where they were to meet for lunch.

Diana and Hunt looked at each other. "Lord Melrose," they said in unison.

11

"What do you know of Lord Melrose?" Diana asked Hunt as they made their way to the pub, trailing only a couple hundred yards behind the man.

Hunt shrugged. "Not much. I've seen him about town and in the halls of parliament, but he is pretty much a nondescript sort of fellow." Of course, Hunt knew from his work with the Home Office that nondescript fellows often made the best spies. But an anarchist? That was quite a stretch for Melrose. As a matter of fact, working with anarchists was a stretch for any peer.

Although it had been Hunt's plan to depart the party as soon as he had the name of the man involved with the nihilists, he found himself reluctant to leave. He'd enjoyed the time spent with Diana and, thus far, he'd been able to keep his lust in check.

Because of their long friendship, he was not surprised to find her witty with a bit of sarcasm regarding the other guests. She was also a stalwart partner in keeping him from being thrust into a situation that would require swift wedding bells.

Although he'd known for years that Diana was a

charming person to spend time with—when she wasn't in trouble, that was—it seemed since her return from Italy, he was enjoying her company even more. But in a much different way. Truth be told, a more dangerous way.

He tried very hard to convince himself that the portrait had nothing to do with this change in attitude. Some days he was close to successful. Was he truly that much of a cad?

There was only one day left of the festivities. The party would end the next night at a ball for all the guests as well as surrounding gentry. Since he'd come this far, he might as well stay to the end and avoid concerns and questions when he took an early leave.

THE FOLLOWING EVENING, Hunt descended the stairs from the bedchambers' level to the ballroom floor. His eyes immediately drifted to where Diana stood with Lady Eunice, who looked pale and insignificant next to Diana, who wore an emerald green satin gown that hugged her curves to perfection. Low in the neckline with slight capped sleeves, the dress had a sparkling netting overlay that draped from Diana's waist to the floor.

Only Diana would dare to wear such a gown. He shook his head at her once again pushing the limits of acceptable apparel for an unmarried young lady. She was surrounded by men, some from the party, and some obviously from those who had been invited from the local gentry.

Annoyed at the attention she was receiving, he made his way across the room, nodding at acquaintances and friends. Now that it was near the end of the party, he was anxious for the event to be over so he could report back to DuBois-Gifford. Hunt had watched Melrose since he'd discovered his perfidy and the man was good. He showed no sense of alarm or guilt. Hunt also noticed that the footman who had met him in the bookstore paid no attention to Melrose while performing his duties.

He elbowed a few of the men surrounding Lady Eunice and Diana, glaring when they neglected to move fast enough. "Good evening, ladies. You both look lovely."

Diana smiled and dipped a curtsey. Lady Eunice giggled and batted her eyelashes.

Hunt reached for Diana's dance card and filled in the first waltz. He wanted to fill all three of them, not wanting to watch her in another man's arms. Which was foolish since he had no claim on her.

He must keep reminding himself of that fact.

Lady Eunice held out her dance card and dangled it in front of him. He took it and penciled in a cotillion. She looked at it and tried very hard not to appear annoyed. He had no intention of encouraging her further by another waltz.

* * *

TRYING NOT TO BE OBVIOUS, Diana studied Hunt as he descended the stairs to the ballroom and could not help but admire the man. His tall, confident demeanor and arrogant stride drew the eyes of just about every woman in the room. Young girls with hope in their eyes, widows and bored matrons with blatant carnal invitations.

He was dressed in all black except for his cravat and silver waistcoat. His light brown hair had been slicked back, but curls were already dropping onto his forehead. But more compelling were his deep brown eyes riveted on her as he made his way across the floor.

"Isn't he wonderful," Lady Eunice sighed.

She tried to hide a smile as Hunt jostled his way

through the group of men surrounding her and Eunice. He looked like a warrior battling for his lady.

He bowed. "Good evening, ladies. You both look lovely." He reached for Diana's dance card and wrote his name. She snuck a peek. A waltz. Could she handle being that close to him for twenty or so minutes?

Lady Eunice immediately dangled her card in front of him and Hunt signed her dance card as well.

They were immediately joined by numerous young ladies fidgeting with their dance cards until Hunt added his name to all. Lady Townsend, a young newly widowed countess, edged between him and one of the debutantes and leaned her impressive breast against his arm, glancing up at him in a way that made Diana quite annoyed.

The contingent of adoring debutantes remained planted firmly in their spots until various gentlemen claimed them for the first dance.

As Mr. Temple claimed Diana, Hunt leaned in, close to her ear. "I will be in the card room."

"Trying to escape your admirers?" She smirked.

He winked. "Just so."

Within a couple of hours, Diana had danced most numbers and was growing quite overheated. She would love a stroll in the garden, but the only one she trusted was Hunt. However, the only time she saw him was when he was dancing with a young lady. True to his word, it appeared he spent his time between dances in the card room.

Lady Eunice walked up to Diana and viewed her with concern. "Oh, heavens, Lady Diana, you look quite spent. Perhaps you will join me for a walk to the ladies retiring room. A maid there will give us a cool cloth, and we can remove our shoes and rest for a while."

Diana checked her dance card. She had two open dances and it would be a good time to take a break. "Yes, that sounds like a wonderful idea."

The two of them linked arms and headed upstairs to the room set aside for the ladies. Lady Eunice was quite chatty as they ascended the stairs. Unusually so.

Several women rested on lounges with lavender scented cloths on their heads. Diana and Eunice found two next to each other and were immediately approached by a maid. She helped them remove their shoes, brought them cups of cool water and cloths for their foreheads.

"This feels wonderful." Diana sighed and closed her eyes. She drifted off to a peaceful place thinking about her upcoming waltz with Hunt. Why did the man plague her so? For years, she'd been comfortable in his presence and never thought of him as any more than a friend.

When had that changed? Now she couldn't seem to be within a few feet of him without her traitorous heart doing stupid things and her stomach swarming with butterflies. She removed her cloth and turned her head to look at Eunice.

Her spot was empty.

Diana frowned and leaned up on one elbow and looked around the room but didn't see her anywhere. Strange. About ten minutes had passed since they'd arrived, but if Eunice had felt refreshed enough to leave, Diana was sure the woman would have let her know.

She shrugged and laid back down. Maybe something came up that required her presence and she had to hurry away.

She returned to her thoughts about Hunt. Suddenly her ruminations were stopped cold when she thought about the possible reason Eunice had left without telling her. A bit panicked, Diana whipped the cloth off her head and sat up to put on her shoes. She waved the maid over. "Did Lady Eunice say where she was going, or leave a message for me?"

"No, my lady." The maid quickly knelt to help Diana with her shoes.

"Thank you," Diana called over her shoulder as she left the room and hurried down the stairs. She thought of all the remarks Eunice had made during the party about Hunt and quickened her footsteps.

She searched the ballroom and the card room. No Hunt and no Eunice. This was not good.

So many couples had been caught together in libraries that Diana decided that was the best place to look. She stopped a footman to ask where the library was located.

Following his directions, she arrived, took a deep breath, and scolded herself for being foolish.

Until she opened the door.

* * *

HUNT STARED at the note in his hand. He'd just been dealt a winning hand and was reluctant to leave the game. But the note from Diana specifically asked him to meet her in the library *immediately.*

He sighed and threw his cards down. "I'm sorry, gentlemen, but I have been summoned." He pushed back his chair and found a footman to direct him.

If Diana was in some sort of trouble again, he would be hard pressed not to throttle her. But he could think of no other reason why she would ask to see him *immediately*.

The library was down a long corridor from the ballroom. The farther he walked from the ballroom, the quieter it became. With a touch of apprehension, he reached the latch and opened the door.

"Diana?" He walked farther into the room and closed the door, lest anyone walk by and see the two of them alone together. "Diana?"

He turned as a rustle of skirts sounded behind him.

"Lady Eunice? Is Lady Diana with you?"

Lady Eunice sauntered up to him, and all his senses went on alert. "Where is Lady Diana?"

Lady Eunice shrugged. "Upstairs in the ladies retiring room."

Feeling foolish since his brain seemed to have shut down, he held out the note. "I received this note to meet her here."

Lady Eunice grew closer until she placed her palms on his chest. "I sent the note." She whispered as if sharing a great secret.

Hunt backed up and walked around her. "If you will excuse me."

She grabbed his arm and pulled him back. "No." She wrapped her arms around his neck and attempted to pull him in for a kiss, but he resisted.

The library door opened, and Diana stepped in. "What the devil is going on in here?"

Lady Eunice growled and turned to Diana. "Lord Huntington and I are having a private conversation. You may leave now."

"No, we're not," Hunt said, taking a deep breath of relief. Who knew Diana would be the one to rescue him this time? He finally pried Lady Eunice's arms from around his neck. "I got a note supposedly from you asking me to meet you here."

Diana walked up to Lady Eunice and took her arm. "May I escort you back to the ballroom, dear? I am sure your guests are missing you."

"No." She attempted to pull her arm free.

"Um, actually, Eunice that was not a question or a request." With a solid grip on her arm, Diana marched the girl firmly toward the door, opened it and pushed her through.

Diana leaned against the closed door and grinned. "Almost got caught, didn't you?"

Hunt walked toward her, and she joined him halfway. He wrapped her in his arms, delight from the near disaster flooding his body. "I can't thank you enough. How did you even know we were here?"

"Eunice invited me to join her in the ladies retiring room. After about ten minutes I noticed she was gone and hadn't said anything to me. At first I didn't think too much about it, but after a while her absence began to concern me.

"When I didn't see you or her in either the ballroom or the card room, I decided my suspicions were valid and since most 'compromises' take place in libraries, I made that my first stop."

Hunt stared down at her. Flushed skin, bright eyes, plump lips ready for kissing. Slowly he bent his head and took her mouth in scorching possession. He'd dreamt of this moment, as well as other more erotic encounters for weeks. Her body pressed against his felt perfect. She fit in all the right places.

He cupped her head and turned it so he could take the kiss deeper, prodding her lips with his tongue. She opened, and he explored her warm, moist mouth. His tongue slid over her teeth and tongue, tasting, sucking. He must be crazy since this would only lead to places he didn't want to go.

Of course he did want to be in those interesting and scandalous places, but this was Diana. Lady Trouble.

His hand seemed to slide up her body of its own volition. He cupped her breast, massaging gently and then slid his finger into the bodice to skim over her already turgid nipple.

They sprang apart as the library door opened.

"What is the meaning of this?" Lady Grafton's loud voice faded, and she gasped when she saw Diana.

Lord Grafton stood alongside her looking confused. "I thought—"

"Never mind, Jasper," Lady Grafton snapped.

Within seconds, it seemed, three other people joined

Lord and Lady Grafton at the door. More gasps and comments followed.

Hunt pulled Diana back to his chest and rested his chin on her head. "Ah, so now it begins."

12

Hunt stared at Lord Grafton who had apparently recovered from the shock of finding their selected victim with Diana in the library instead of their daughter. He now apparently decided to portray the insulted host who had to handle the apparent scandal.

"Lady Diana, who is responsible for you with your father residing out in South Yorkshire?" Lord Grafton barely got the words out with his wife glaring at him as if the debacle was his fault.

Lady Grafton turned her glare to Diana. Obviously she, her husband and Lady Eunice had all been involved in an attempt to trap him into wedlock. Although they'd failed, Hunt mused, he was still staring at the parson's noose.

With Diana.

Lady Trouble.

The woman he'd lusted after for weeks.

He released Diana, and she turned to face Lord and Lady Grafton. She lifted her chin. "I am responsible for myself, my lord."

Lady Grafton waved her hand in dismissal. "Nonsense. Every woman must have a man responsible for her. It will be necessary for Lord Huntington to visit with your father, which would be quite a trip if there is no one closer."

"Again, Lady Grafton, I do not mean to be rude, but I am responsible for myself," Diana responded, her voice laced with anger.

Lord Denbigh, one of the men who had gathered at the doorway to view the current calamity, stepped into the room and looked condescendingly at Diana. "As a dear friend of your father, my lady, I am quite certain the Marquess of Rockingham would be pleased to have me step into his place and deal with Lord Huntington."

Diana closed her eyes and groaned. "May I please have a few moments to speak with Lord Huntington?"

"You've already caused enough trouble, gel," Lady Grafton said. "I will not allow this scandal to continue by allowing the two of you alone. Lord only knows what you are up to."

Hunt stepped away from Diana, the blood pounding in his chest at the insult to her. There must have been something in his expression that terrorized the woman because she moved behind her husband. As if he would strike a lady. But he would have no trouble taking out Lord Grafton.

"I advise you to not speak to my fiancée in that manner, my lady."

"Fiancée!" Several people—including Diana—gasped.

"Yes, sweetheart." He directed his comments to a very pale Diana. "I know we wished to keep it a secret until we returned to London, but it seems the cat was let out of the bag." Hunt turned to the group at the doorway, wrapping his arm around Diana's shoulders. "Since Lady Diana has just now accepted my hand in marriage, I assume you will all wish us happy."

A few 'best wishes' and 'wish you wells' drifted over the group.

Lady Grafton narrowed her eyes. "I don't know what you are trying to pull off here, Lord Huntington, but I had better see a wedding in the near future or your so-called fiancée will be totally disgraced."

She had the nerve to wag her finger at Diana. "No running off to Italy this time to ward off a scandal, gel."

Hunt had had enough of the banter and nonsense that Lady Grafton herself had started. He cursed himself for not considering that if Lady Eunice had planned to have it look as though he'd compromised her, arrangements would have been made to have someone 'find' him and the young lady alone in the library.

Although he would be eternally grateful he'd not been found with Lady Eunice, he still had a problem on his hands. Lady Grafton was correct. Diana had no choice this time. She had to marry or be forever banned from the *ton*.

And that left him with a woman he dreamt many a night having in his bed, but never had he thought to have to deal with her as his wife.

His wife.

Blasted hell. Lady Trouble was all his.

Diana turned to him and lowered her voice, which wasn't entirely necessary since the crowd at the doorway had doubled in size and their voices would cover the sound of an uprising at Newgate. "Hunt, I have to get out of here. I can't breathe."

"Come." He moved her forward and the crowd began to divide. "My fiancée and I have had enough celebration for one evening. If you will excuse us."

Before anyone could recover enough to stop them, they made their way through the group. Hunt directed Diana past the ballroom, which amazingly enough still held quite a few people, and into a small drawing room that he'd noticed before had a French door to the patio.

* * *

DIANA TOOK a deep breath of the fresh air from the garden which helped to fade the black dots in her eyes. Then she began to shiver, the chill coming from deep inside. Hunt removed his jacket and placed it gently over her shoulders.

"Thank you." It warmed her both inside and out. The light scent of bay rum emanated from the jacket, reminding her that this time she was not alone in disaster. No, somehow she had managed to drag her lifelong rescuer into her mess.

She stared out over the shrubbery, her thoughts so convoluted she was starting to feel the beginning of a megrim. Best to get this over with before the headache hit her full force and she had to go to bed. She took a deep breath. "I appreciate you attempting to save me once again, Hunt, but you do realize we cannot marry. Not each other, anyway."

He studied her for a minute. "There is no choice here, Diana."

"There are always choices. Admit it. You would never marry me unless you were forced."

He ran his fingers through his hair. "That's not true."

She rolled her eyes. "Please. I thought I could at least count on honesty from you."

"I am being honest." He pulled her into his arms, his eyes boring into her, making parts of her body she generally ignored come to life. "I must admit I can't stop thinking about taking you to my bed ever since I saw that portrait."

Despite the arousal his words were doing to her insides, Diana glared at him. "I will dismiss for now my request that you not look at the portrait and point out that lust is not a reason for marriage."

He threw his head back and laughed. "Is that what you were taught in the schoolroom? Perhaps marriages of convenience or forced marriages might not be for lust only, but otherwise I am sure most grooms lust after their brides."

She pulled away from him, giving herself some space. She couldn't think when he was close like that. "Hunt. *This* is a forced marriage. Or should I say it would be a forced marriage if we went through with it."

"Diana, we cannot *not* go through with it. You will be ruined."

She waved her hand. "I've been ruined like this before and survived."

"I would hardly call running off to Italy for a year surviving. If you refuse my offer of marriage it will be the second time that happened. There will be no recovering from it this time."

They both remained silent for several moments. Then Hunt said, "This is my fault anyway."

Diana's brows rose. "How did you come to that conclusion since I followed you into the library? And it was a note supposedly from me that drew you there."

Hunt shook his head. "You saved me from potential hell. If you hadn't followed me into the library, it would be Lady Eunice and me having this conversation right now." He shuddered. "I can't imagine the horror of being tied to her for the rest of my life."

Diana smirked. "Yet you can imagine being tied to Lady Trouble for the rest of your life?"

He frowned. "Where did you hear that?"

She walked away from him and wrapped her arms around herself trying to sort out this newest muddle. She couldn't think when he was near. "Oh, come now, Hunt. Certainly you don't think that such a moniker has slipped by me?" She waved him off. "I've known about that for ages."

Hunt drew himself up, a bit of arrogance and, surprisingly, a bit of uncertainty in his visage. "Perhaps *you* don't wish to marry *me*."

Had he asked that question a few weeks ago she would have easily said, *No I don't want to marry you. We would never suit.* He'd been no more than her friend, confidant and savior all her life.

Until recently.

Then everything seemed to change, and she found herself thinking about him in ways she never had before. She considered how it would feel to have his warm large hands on her naked flesh, fondling, caressing, stroking and how far things would have gone when he kissed her in the library if Lord and Lady Grafton had not shown up.

Perhaps she was Lady Trouble after all because she doubted if she would have stopped him.

"Truthfully, I have not given marrying you much thought because I was certain you would never have offered for me unless forced." She shrugged. "Which, I guess, is exactly what has happened."

Hunt held out his hand. "Diana. Come here."

For some reason that soft request had her heart thumping double time. She took his hand, and he drew her into his arms. "I don't want you to think of this as a forced marriage. It's a necessity."

"Is there a difference?"

"Yes. Marrying Lady Eunice would be forced. Marrying you is a necessity."

"I don't think it makes a dif—" Her words were cut off when he covered her mouth with his. A swarm of butterflies entered her stomach, and her knees felt weaker than when she'd first seen Lord and Lady Grafton glaring at the two of them in the library.

No black dots, however.

Those were her last thoughts as Hunt turned the kiss into something feral and greedy. He plunged into her mouth with his tongue and pulled her even closer.

She moved her hands up his arms and encircled his

neck, playing with the soft strands of hair curling over his cravat.

"Say yes, Diana," he mumbled as his mouth swept over her jaw, kissing and nipping. "Say yes." His lips moved to the soft sensitive skin behind her ear. His warm mint and brandy scented breath added goose flesh to her skin, combining with her already erratic heartbeat and fluttering stomach.

"I can't."

"Yes. You can." He took her mouth again, this time adding all the arrogance and loftiness that was the Earl of Huntington into the kiss.

She was dizzy. Her knees buckled, and she would have slipped to his feet had he not gripped her so powerfully against his hard body. She needed air, she needed time to think, to step away. Her hands came to his chest and she pushed.

Being the gentleman that he was, Hunt released her and moved back, but kept her lightly in his hold. "What's wrong?"

"I need time to think, Hunt. Marriage is a serious business. I truly don't believe you would be happy married to me. If you're not happy, then I won't be happy. We could spend the rest of our lives making each other miserable."

He released her and took her hand, moving them to a small table against the balustrade. After pulling out a chair for her and settling across from her, he took her hands and covered them with his, resting them on the table. "I had planned to marry this year."

She grinned. "Not me."

"You must marry sometime, Diana. You were not made for spinsterhood. You are a warm, loving woman. You would make a wonderful mother."

"And a wife?" Her smile dissolved. "That might be so, but I would have favored being courted and escorted to the theater and balls, and museums. I would have preferred to have a man on bended knee asking for my hand."

He lifted their joint hands. "I have your hand."

She pulled it back and laughed. "Not yet."

"Very well. We will continue to have everyone believe we are betrothed. However, I will court you. If after a few weeks you decide we will not suit, we will quietly announce we have changed our minds and go our merry ways."

Her eyes grew wide. "Do you think that would work?"

"We will make it work. I have no doubt that we will suit, but I want you to be sure."

She shook her head. "What I am sure about, my lord, is that you must have had way too much brandy before you headed to the library to meet me." She tilted her head and looked him in the eye. "And I don't believe it has yet worn off."

13

"Melrose, eh?" Sir Phillip DuBois-Gifford stood straight, his hands clasped behind his back as he stared out the window of his office, facing nothing but a gray sky, drizzles of rain and a near-crumbling building across the way.

"Yes, sir," Hunt said, sitting on a chair in front of the man's desk that seemed ready to collapse under his weight. "There is a possibility we were incorrect, but I saw no reason for a footman to be meeting with a lord in a bookstore."

DuBois-Gifford swung around. "We? Was someone with you at the time?"

"Yes, sir. I was accompanied by my betrothed at the time."

"Betrothed? When did this happen, Huntington?"

Hunt shifted, not comfortable with the look Sir Phillip cast in his direction. "Actually, sir, Lady Diana and I became engaged at the house party."

"Lady Diana Pemberton? Rockingham's daughter?"

"Yes, sir. Is there a problem here?" He might as well face whatever the man's concern was immediately.

He studied Hunt with a piercing look that reminded him of his tutors in school when he fell behind in his work. "Is she not the young lady who has barely escaped several scandals? Did she not retire to Italy for a year due to some debacle?"

Hunt being surprised by Sir Phillip's knowledge of Diana's escapades was utter foolishness on his part. No one did the sort of work the man did and directed others to do without knowing just about everything about everyone.

Hunt lowered his voice, trying hard to keep the anger in check at Sir Phillip's words. If the man used the term Lady Trouble, Hunt might be driven to flatten him. "Lady Diana did spend about a year in Italy visiting her mother's family."

To Hunt's relief, DuBois-Gifford waved it off and moved to his chair behind his desk. "I will need some documentation to connect Melrose to this movement."

"What information have you already?" Hunt asked.

"About five years ago, a woman by the name of Miss Charlotte Wilson started an anarchist newsletter, humorously entitled *Freedom*. We have reason to believe she has more than enough followers to actually stage a good attempt to overthrow the government."

Hunt blew out a low whistle.

"Miss Wilson has been favoring a violent revolution, and I'm afraid she has more than one man of high power on her side."

"And the Home Office's stance on this?" Hunt asked.

"Some are believers, some skeptics, claiming we are panicking for naught. However, the Crown is concerned and has asked me to delve into it further. That is why I need whatever paperwork Melrose might have. If we can get names, we have a good chance of quelling any revolution before it starts, and the resulting panic that would hit the general public."

Hunt rose when DuBois-Gifford stood and offered his hand, his signal that the meeting was over. "I expect to hear from you as soon as you are able."

"Yes, sir." Hunt nodded and left the office. Deep in thought, he strode down the corridor and out the door. He waved his carriage forward and climbed in, grateful that the rain had temporarily subsided.

The ride home took longer than necessary because of traffic and wet streets. It gave Hunt time to consider the present state of his life. Betrothed to Diana. The annoyance that swelled up in him at DuBois-Gifford's comments gave him pause.

Would he be defending Diana's name for the rest of his life? Would he have to endure jokes and snide remarks in his clubs? What he really needed to examine was his easy acceptance of their forced betrothal and coming wedding.

He knew without a doubt that, at one time, he would have been horrified to find himself betrothed to Diana.

Although she had not yet agreed. But she was not a stupid woman and would come to realize if she wanted to maintain any standing in Society whatsoever, she must marry him.

Only months ago, he might have been tempted to challenge his honor and packed up and left the country rather than marry the woman, but things had changed. Oh, the portrait and seeing her in all her glory—he still wondered if the artist got it right—had certainly began his shift from 'annoying-always-in-trouble-friend', to thinking of her as a desirable woman who was witty, strong, and had a mind of her own.

All the things that were not on his list of qualities for potential brides.

She was also compassionate and caring. As he'd stated to her, she would be a wonderful mother. He enjoyed her company and found himself searching for her at every event and looking forward to holding her in his arms while they waltzed.

Was that love? Hardly. But he thought there was a possibility that they could have a strong marriage.

The rain had started up again by the time the carriage arrived at his house. Rather than wait for the driver to climb down with an umbrella, Hunt hopped from the carriage and took the steps two at a time to the front door.

"Where is Marcus?" Hunt asked as he shrugged out of his wet coat and handed it off to the butler. "Tell him I need to see him in my bedchamber post haste."

"Yes, my lord."

Once he reached his room, he grabbed a piece of linen and dried his hair. He was already out of his wet clothes when the valet appeared. "My lord, how can I be of service?"

"I need some of your expertise."

The man nodded. He'd done several things for Hunt in the past that didn't fall into the realm of valet. Marcus had been raised on the streets and, after a near-death experience, managed to get a job at a tailor shop, taking out the trash and cleaning up. He watched and learned and accosted Hunt on the street after leaving the tailor shop one afternoon and asked for a job.

Impressed with the young man's ambition and willingness to learn, he agreed to take him on as an assistant to Sergio, his former valet who was growing close to his pension. Two years later, Sergio retired and Marcus took over full duties.

"I need to examine some papers in Lord Melrose's house."

Marcus never batted an eye.

"I prefer not to crawl through the window like a burglar. I want you to find someone in Melrose's household who will leave the back door open for a price."

"Yes, my lord. That will not be a problem. I can think of a couple already."

Another of Marcus's talents was helping former street urchins gain respectable employment. He had several male and female friends in great houses all over London.

While these cohorts were, for the most part, honest, they were always up for a little extra coin.

"Excellent. Just let me know what night."

Whistling now that the unpleasant part of the day was over, Hunt headed to his office where the safe holding the family jewels were kept.

He'd been barely out of university when his father had passed away, only months after his mother. He'd taken on the responsibility of his two brothers and was grateful when they came to him with the request to help finance The Rose Room.

The family jewels had been passed down for generations. Hunt had never examined them, since they were meant to go to his wife and, until now, she'd been an elusive, shadowy woman.

Since now there was a face—and a figure—attached to this mystery woman, he pulled the box out of the safe with the idea of finding something that would suit Diana.

His soon to be wife.

Maybe.

What amazed him was how quickly he'd accepted Diana as his. What also amazed him was why it had taken him this long, and another misstep, to realize how much he wanted her. Had probably always wanted her. Even before he saw the portrait.

There were two types of *perfect* wives. The young debutantes who had been raised to never speak out, always agree, lay very still in bed until *it* was all over, produce perfect heirs while praying her husband was then done with the 'nasty' business, and run an efficient household.

Then there was a woman who was perfect for him.

Lady Diana Pemberton.

He selected what he thought would be the perfect ring for her. It was a black onyx surrounded by small diamonds. It seemed to be about the correct size, but that could be altered.

The question was, would she accept it?

* * *

DIANA LIFTED her skirts as Marguerite helped her slide her slippers on. She straightened when that was finished and regarded herself in the mirror. The pale, rose gown with silver scrolls across the top and around the short capped sleeves had always been one of her favorites.

She leaned closer to the mirror and examined her face. In Italy, she had learned about Pear's Almond Bloom, all the rage at the time, but once she returned to London, where the air was more moist, she decided her complexion looked better without the powder unless she was hiding anxiety.

Shaking her head back and forth, she smiled at the earbobs that caught the light next to the dressing table. She quickly stood. Whyever was she so concerned with how she looked tonight?

Simple. Because Hunt was escorting her to the theater, the first of their outings to mark the beginning of their courtship.

She grinned. Yes, they'd been caught in a compromising situation, but in all the disasters she'd been involved in and needed Hunt's rescue, this was one they were in together.

Diana scooped up her shawl and reticule from the blue and white striped chair near the door to her bedroom. "I will be late, I am sure, since most likely we will stop for a late supper after the theater."

"Then I shall rest on the small bed here in the

room." Marguerite had her own room one floor above, but on the evenings Diana expected to be late, the girl slept on the cot so she could help her mistress out of her clothing and then retire to her own room.

Deciding a sherry would be welcomed while waiting for Hunt, she made her way to the drawing room. Since she was supposedly 'betrothed' she no longer found it necessary to have Mrs. Strickland accompany her everywhere.

Not wanting to leave the poor—but annoying—woman without employment, Diana had arranged for her to be companion to elderly Lady Winborne, a long-time friend of Diana's grandmama.

She downed the last of her sherry when the door knocker sounded, and she heard Hunt's voice. She closed her eyes at the sliver of anticipation that glided over her. This was ridiculous. She would not allow herself to be affected by the man.

With a shaky hand—blast it—she placed the sherry glass on the table and smiled as he entered the room.

Men like the Earl of Huntington should be against the law. Uncommonly handsome, his deep brown eyes twinkled with mirth as he viewed her. Did she look so very amusing then?

His well-tailored suit fit him like a comfortable soft leather glove. His silk pure white ascot set off the warmth of his skin. He approached her with his hand extended. She raised her hand, and he took it, turned her hand to place a kiss with his warm lips on the sensitive skin of her wrist. Whyever hadn't she put her gloves on already?

She curled her hand and cursed the rush of heat that rose to her face. "Would you care for a drink, my lord?"

Hunt laughed softly.

Refusing to allow him to view her as unsettled by his presence, she raised her chin. "A drink?"

"Yes, sweetheart. I will pour myself a brandy. We

have some time. Why don't you sit and I will bring you another"—he looked at her glass—"sherry?"

"Yes."

Taking a deep breath, she settled on the most uncomfortable piece of furniture in the room, a red flowered settee that had been a favorite of grandmama. Perhaps the discomfort would keep her sharp so she didn't make a fool of herself.

Hunt sat next to her and took a sip of his brandy, then removed the glass of sherry from her hand and placed it on the table next to his. "I have something for you."

Again her heart began to race. "What is it?" She licked her dry lips.

He withdrew a beautiful black onyx ring with over a dozen small diamonds surrounding it from his pocket. She regarded him with raised eyebrows.

"A betrothal ring from the Huntington family jewel collection."

14

Hunt's stomach dropped as Diana continued to stare at the ring as if it possessed the power to destroy her. "Is something wrong?"

She jumped up. "I thought the plan was to court for a while and then discuss a betrothal."

He reached up and pulled her back down alongside him. "Diana, you have been compromised. Again. And what of my honor? When the situation happened with Lord Stratford last year you escaped to Italy, but he was shunned for quite a while for not doing the honorable thing."

"Why? He tried to get me to marry him, but since that was his plan all along—to compromise me—I refused. But he did offer, so he should not have been shunned."

"It matters not, Diana. You were both involved in the scandal and, although the man's part in it is never as serious as the woman's they still feel the brunt of the *ton* turning their backs on them."

"I see." She stiffened and glared at him. "First it was *a necessity* for us to marry, and now it's about *your honor*. Quite romantic. I'm afraid you need lessons, my lord, in how to woo a young lady."

Hunt slumped and ran his fingers through his hair. He replayed in his mind why he had decided Diana was the best woman for him. It was inevitable. From the time he first rescued her from a tree with a dog snapping at her heels, to stealing the portrait, he'd known deep inside that despite his desire to have a biddable, demure, never-a-scandal wife, Diana was the one who had always held his heart.

However, given the circumstances in which they found themselves, she would never believe it. The simple fact was she didn't trust him and, given his attitude toward her, she had good reason. If he wanted a happy wife—and he would have Diana—one who didn't feel like a penance, it was up to him to convince her.

He reached over and took her hands in his. "My insistence on marriage is much more than a necessity, or my honor." He squeezed her hands as she made an unladylike sound and attempted to pull her hands away. "I know you don't believe that and, given our history, I don't blame you. Therefore, I ask that you wear this ring, not as an official betrothal, but the need to stem further gossip and nasty comments when we go out and about in Society.

"And, going out and about in Society is vital if we're to save both our reputations. However, I know what our plan is, you know what it is—to wait and see if we suit, or whatever it is that is holding you back, but that will remain our secret. To the world, we are a happily engaged couple." He held the ring out once more. "Will you wear it under those conditions?"

Diana looked down at the ring and then back at him again. Something in his eyes must have touched her since her demeanor shifted and she offered him a slight smile. "You can be quite the eloquent speaker when the situation calls for it, my lord." She chewed on her lower lip for a few moments. "Very well. I will accept the ring under those conditions."

He slid it on her finger. The ring was a tad big, but he would have it adjusted. Right now he was merely grateful that she'd accepted.

He rubbed his thumb over her knuckles. "Perhaps a kiss to seal our betrothal?"

"Pretend betrothal," she returned.

He smiled at her stubbornness and reached out to cup her chin. Her skin was soft, like satin petals on a rose. He leaned in and gently touched his lips to hers. She didn't pull back, so he wrapped his arm around her and pulled her close, taking the kiss deeper.

Nudging her lips, his tongue swept in, teasing, tasting, taking possession. A slight moan from Diana had him pulling back, kissing the soft skin under her ear, along her jaw and neck. "So sweet."

She pressed closer, her breasts crushed against his chest. In her naivety, she was unaware of how her moans and movements were nudging him past where he planned to stop. "I want you, Diana. I have for so long."

She shook her head. "Not true. You've thought of me as the plague for years."

"I love plagues." He returned to her mouth, his hand sliding up her ribs to cup her breast. There wasn't much he could do with her layers of clothing hampering him, but she picked that moment to pull back anyway.

They were both panting, and her face was flushed. She cleared her throat and patted her hair. "I believe it is time to leave."

Since she was right, and he shouldn't be leading her down the path where marriage would be inevitable instead of necessary, he stood and held out his hand.

And sat right back down when he realized the bit of passion they'd shared had awakened body parts of which he did not want her aware. Not yet, at least.

"Finish your drink." He motioned to her glass and

downed his own drink. Since Diana sipped at hers, it gave him enough time to recover his dignity to stand and appear the gentleman.

* * *

DIANA TURNED as Hunt placed the rose-colored lace shawl that matched her gown over her shoulders. Her breathing had finally returned to normal, but she was still shaken by their kiss.

Not that it was the first kiss they'd shared, but this one shocked her. Perhaps it was wearing the betrothal ring. Or maybe it was feeling things for her long-time friend she'd never felt before.

She'd known her feelings toward Hunt had changed since her return from Italy. No. That wasn't quite true. It wasn't until he'd viewed the portrait and his attitude changed toward her that she found herself viewing him in a different light.

They made their way down the steps to his waiting carriage. Hunt helped her in and took the seat across from her. Facing backward. Always the gentleman.

"Hunt, can we be honest?" The vehicle started up, and she grabbed the strap hanging alongside her as they hit a rut in the road.

His eyebrows rose. "Of course."

"What are your thoughts on an ideal wife?"

Hunt had the nerve to throw his head back and laugh. "Oh, no. You're not going to drag me into that."

She stiffened at his annoying reaction to an honest question. "I don't intend to drag you into anything. I just want to know how far removed I am from what you had wanted for a wife. This was your year to find a bride, and I had no reason to believe you would ever look in my direction. Am I right?"

He rested his foot on his knee and stared at her for a

moment. "What I thought I wanted and what I actually need turned out to be two different things."

She huffed. "Whatever does that nebulous statement mean?"

"'Tis not so nebulous. I will admit I've always wanted a biddable young lady. But, to be honest, every biddable young lady I met so far this Season was boring as hell. Excuse my language."

She waved him off. "No matter."

Hunt leaned forward, resting his forearms on his thighs. "You see. That is precisely what I mean. Can you imagine Lady Eunice or anyone of her ilk not fainting dead away at my use of the word 'hell'?"

"All right. Then an ideal wife is one who allows cussing?"

He grinned. "That was not what I meant, and you are intelligent enough to know that. Which is another reason I think we would suit. You are a smart, witty, knowledgeable woman. You have traveled, lived on your own. Our conversations involve more than the color of your ribbon choices or how well you play the pianoforte."

"I don't play very well, I'm afraid."

"That is perhaps why you don't mention it." He reached across the open space and took her hand. "It turns out what I need and what I want are not the same thing. I need you."

"Ah, but do you want me?"

He released her hand and sat back. "You have no idea how much I want you, Diana."

The look on his face, the hooded eyes and the slight tilt of his lips had her lady parts throbbing. Despite her best efforts, a flush rose from her middle to cover her upper body. Thank goodness the carriage was dark so he couldn't see her blush.

Diana folded her hands in her lap and leaned against the squab, staring at her entwined fingers. Another ten minutes of silence passed as she considered what Hunt said. He sounded sincere which astonished as well as frightened her. Was she ready to accept a marriage between them? Would he grow tired of her constant ability to find trouble? On the other hand, was she willing to change herself to suit the title of Countess?

Her brain in a whirl enough to give her a megrim, she used a finger to move aside the curtain. "It appears we're almost there."

As she gathered her things, they came to a rolling stop, and the driver jumped down to open the door. Hunt stepped out first and turned to help Diana out of the carriage. She took his extended hand, and a sharp jolt ran up her arm, and her eyes flicked to his. He must have felt the same thing, but instead of surprised, he looked pleased.

Whatever was he all about? Hunt was turning into a mystery. He'd gone from eschewing the idea of marriage—at least to her anyway—to attempting to talk her into it. She was more confused than ever.

She took his arm, and they climbed the steps to the theater. She was excited to see Charles Dickens' *Oliver Twist,* a book she'd read many times over and was anxious to see all the characters come to life.

"Good evening, Lady Diana, Lord Huntington." Lady Torrington gazed at them through her looking glass. The old gossipmonger looked pointedly at Diana's left hand. "Ah, I heard you two had gotten yourselves betrothed, but knowing this young man as I do," she tapped Hunt on this arm with her fan, "I doubted he would choose *you* for a bride."

Diana felt Hunt's muscles stiffen under her arm. Hopefully, he was not about to make a scene since the last thing they needed was more notoriety. She jumped in. "Isn't it lovely when one can surprise one's peers?"

Hunt made a noise that could only be a construed as a meager suppression of laughter.

"You've always been a sharp gel." The older woman looked between Diana and Hunt. "I believe you two will suit. I hope to be around long enough to see the offspring you produce." With those words, she winked, then turned and hobbled away.

"For a moment I thought we were in trouble, there," Hunt said as they continued their stroll around the lobby.

Thinking of the tension she'd felt in his arm, she said, "I believe Lady Torrington enjoys those who stand up to her. But then, I feel her attitude would have been different had you answered her."

Hunt nodded. "You are correct. No one insults my fiancée."

"Pretend fiancée," she muttered.

"Well, look who is strolling the halls of Drury Lane." Hunt's brother, Driscoll stepped in front of them, a lovely young lady clinging to his arm.

Hunt slapped Driscoll on the back, who returned the favor, both of them grinning. "Why aren't you working?" Hunt asked.

"I am permitted one night a week off and this is it." He turned to the young lady. "Miss Davenport, may I present my high in the instep brother, the Earl of Huntington and Lady Diana Pemberton."

"My fiancée," Hunt added.

Driscoll's brows reached his hairline. "When did this happen?"

"Recently."

"It is lovely to meet you both," Miss Davenport said. "Mr. Rose has told me so much about you, my lord."

"Don't believe everything he says." The brothers grinned at each other again.

"What a surprise. The infamous couple from the Grafton House Party." Lord Melrose bowed and smiled at the two of them, something in his eyes making Diana uncomfortable. But then, the man was a member of the peerage who consorted with anarchists.

Hopefully he hadn't sought them out because of what they'd uncovered at the house party.

She gulped when he said, "There is something I wish to speak with you about, Hunt."

15

Two nights after the trip to the theater, Hunt entered The Rose Room and took the stairs two at a time to the office floor. He strode down the corridor and pushed open the door to see Driscoll bent over his ledgers and Dante slumped in a chair, his feet on the desk.

"Don't you ever work?" he asked his younger brother. "Every time I come here, you're sitting on your arse."

"Good evening to you, too, brother. It just so happens I'm on a break."

"You're always on a break." Hunt pushed Dante's feet off the desk and pulled up a chair, turning it around and sitting with his arms folded over the back. "I have an issue with which I need your help."

Driscoll put his pencil down, took off his spectacles, and rubbed his eyes with his index finger and thumb. "What do you need?"

"I assume Lord Melrose is a patron of The Rose Room?"

Dante snorted. "Patron isn't a strong enough word. It's to the point where I'm thinking we should start charging him rent."

"Except he loses so much money to us we can afford to bring in a bed for him." Driscoll leaned back and crossed his arms over his chest.

"Good, that's what I was hoping to hear."

Dante leaned forward, his sluggish attitude gone. "Why the interest in Melrose and his sad state of affairs?"

Despite his indolent demeanor, Dante Rose was sharp-witted and intelligent. He'd made honors in all his subjects at University and still found time to bed a sufficient number of women and drag several of his friends home after a night of drinking and carousing. His mathematical near-genius had made The Rose Room the most successful gambling hell in all of London, probably England as well.

"According to DuBois-Gifford, Melrose is involved with anarchists."

Driscoll let out with a low whistle.

"I confirmed that information for Sir Phillip when I attended the Grafton house party. DuBois-Gifford had information that the peer working with the anarchists would be at the house party and would be either passing along information or gaining information from one of the staff members.

"Diana and I saw Melrose with one of the footmen at the bookstore in the small village near Grafton Manor. They were conversing in a secretive manner. After that encounter, they completely ignored each other for the remainder of the party."

Dante leaned back and stretched. "This wouldn't be the Lady Diana to whom I understand you've become betrothed? Our Lady Diana? The one who—"

"Stop." Hunter glared at his youngest brother. "We are not discussing my fiancée. And I suggest you keep any derisive comments to yourself."

Dante smirked and raised his hands, palms forward.

"As you say, big brother. I merely wanted to wish you both well."

Hunt snorted and continued. "Another point in this story is J. D. Mallory whose body was found in his burned-out studio. He didn't die from the fire, but the two bullet holes in his chest. The man was apparently working with the group and planned on escaping to the continent. Why he was fleeing, I have no idea, but he might have been absconding with either money, information, or names. Perhaps all three."

The men remained silent for a moment, then Hunt added, "I saw Melrose at the theater the other night, and he approached me about speaking with the two of you about extending him more credit." He turned to Driscoll. "Apparently he has been cut off?"

"Yes. He has."

"Here is where my favor from the two of you comes in. I have been asked by Sir Phillip to slip into Melrose's house and gather whatever documentation I can regarding his involvement. I have guaranteed access to the house, but I need to make sure he doesn't return before I finish."

Dante glanced over at Driscoll. "How bad is Melrose's account?"

"Bad enough, but we can certainly keep him busy enough here without adding too much to his debt."

Driscoll turned to Hunt. "When?"

"That I must get back to you on. My valet has a contact with someone at Melrose's house who will leave the back door open for me. We just need to coordinate with him, then I'll know the day. How can we be sure Melrose will be here that night?"

Driscoll tapped the end of his pencil on the table. "Easy enough. He is currently banned, but I can send around a note that you spoke with us, and he is now allowed back in with a limited amount of credit. I can practically guarantee he will arrive the very night I send the note."

Hunt slapped his hands on his thighs and stood. "Good. Let me know when the note goes out. Give me a few days to set it up with my man." He moved toward the door.

"Wait," Dante said, his annoying grin putting Hunt on alert. "When is the wedding?"

"We haven't set a date yet."

"Ah, some doubts on your part, perhaps?" Dante laughed. "Not that I am suggesting anything about the young lady's past."

Hunt glared at his youngest brother. "No. Actually the reticence is on Lady Diana's part." With a quick two-finger salute, he left the room with his brothers' startled expressions on their faces and headed out of the club.

"WHERE IS MARCUS?" Hunt asked as he handed his hat and gloves to Peters, the man at the door. Another one of Marcus's recruits.

"The last time I saw him, my lord, he was headed to the kitchen."

Most likely to cajole Cook out of one of her apple pasties. The man had an enormous sweet tooth.

Hunt made his way to the kitchen where, as expected, Marcus was charming the cook, who, despite her age was giggling like a schoolgirl. "Marcus!"

He turned to Hunt. "Yes, my lord."

"Grab your pastie and attend me in the library." Hunt winked at Cook and left the room.

Marcus came through the doorway, swallowing the last of his treat. "What do you need, my lord?"

Hunt waved to the seat in front of his desk. "I need you to contact your man at Melrose's house and work out a date he will leave the back door unlocked."

"Any particular day?"

"Nothing specific but give me a day or two to work things out."

* * *

DIANA JOINED Hunt in her drawing room where he waited to escort her on a drive through Hyde Park. It was the fashionable hour for members of the *ton* to see and be seen.

Hunt walked up to her and took her hand in his. Turning her hand, he kissed the sensitive skin on the inside of her wrist. She flushed at the reaction her body had to that intimate contact.

"You look lovely, Diana."

"Thank you." She'd been quite pleased with the reflection in her mirror before she'd left her room. The yellow chiné was one of her favorites. The neckline was higher than one would expect to wear to an evening event, but quite appropriate for a ride in the park.

The deeper yellow flowered embroidery lining the long sleeves and bottom of the gown gave it a more elegant look than a normal carriage dress. The gown hugged her waist and stomach with the back drawn into a fashionable bow on her lower back. The lovely yellow satin hat with netting tied under her chin was set off by a daisy trim along the edging of the piece.

Fumbling slightly with the raw admiration in Hunt's eyes, she pulled on her gloves. The heat in her face was unnerving. "I am ready," she said.

They left the house and made their way down to Hunt's open-air carriage. "I decided to bring a driver along today so we can freely converse." Hunt helped her up into the vehicle where they sat side by side. The lovely scent of bay rum drifted to her nose from Hunt's close proximity.

Diana snapped open her parasol and rested the shaft

on her shoulder. "It's truly a beautiful day for a drive, Hunt. I'm so glad you suggested it."

He studied her so carefully, she grew uncomfortable. "What?"

Hunt shook his head. "Nothing. I was just thinking how very beautiful you are, Diana. I don't think I say it often enough."

She waved her hand, feeling the rising of another blush to her face. "Oh, please. I am no more than ordinary." She'd never been vain but was certainly aware of her appeal to the male species. For some reason, however, Hunt's very sincere comment both pleased and disquieted her.

He took her hand in his and linked their fingers. "There is nothing ordinary about you, sweeting."

Wishing to move the subject off herself, she said, "I believe you were to meet with your Home Office contact after our return from Grafton Manor. With all that happened, I've forgotten to ask you about it. Did you pass your information along?"

Hunt shifted to rest his foot on his knee, giving Diana much needed breathing space. "I did. Sir Phillip was quite pleased with the information I was able to pass along to him."

"What next? Did he say what he would do?"

He placed his arm across the back of the seat and leaned in close. "Yes. Sir Phillip has commissioned me to search Melrose's house for documentation he can take to the Prime Minister."

Diana's eyes grew wide. "How very exciting. How do you plan to do that?"

He sat back. "Arrangements that you need not concern yourself with are in play. I hope to have it all finished and be done with the entire matter by next week. We do have a wedding to plan."

"Um, just a minute. We are not planning a wedding.

I accepted this ring with the condition that we would court for a while and see if we suited."

"We are courting. We've been to the theater and now on a drive through Hyde Park."

"Two events does not a courtship make."

"Darling, we have been friends most of our lives. The purpose of courtship is for the man and woman to learn about each other. I doubt there is anything about you I don't know, and vice versa."

She shifted so she could share her displeasure by glaring at him. "Are you going back on our deal, my lord?"

"No. Yes. I don't know. I keep hearing rumors and comments, and I don't like what I'm hearing. I hate to revisit the subject again, Diana, but we have very little choice in this matter." He placed his knuckle under her chin and tilted her head up. "What are your reservations? Truly. I want to hear them."

Diana looked out the side of the carriage. They were growing close to Hyde Park and no conversation would be private once they arrived. "I don't want to be a man's penance. I don't want to be married to someone who is always waiting to see what trouble I will get into next. I don't want a marriage where I am considered a fumbling, troublesome woman. Someone who will never be a true partner because she has to be watched and guarded at all times, lest she lose one of the children, or burn down the house."

"We will have a nanny to watch the children."

She turned back to him. "This is not funny, Hunt. You know deep in your heart you never wanted to marry me. I will not be a wife, but an albatross."

"Stop. And wait just a minute. I've let you go a bit too far with this. You are not my penance or an albatross. I agree that marrying you was not in my original plans, but plans change." He placed his hands on her shoulders and turned her toward him. "I want this,

Diana. Not because I'm being forced, but because I want *you*. You with all your faults, foibles and propensity for getting into trouble."

"Why?" She was genuinely confused.

"Because I have come to realize the type of woman I thought I wanted bores me to death. One thing I can say about you, sweetheart, is there will never be a boring moment in my life."

"And that is enough?"

"Yes. That is enough. Well, aside from the fact that I desire you so much I cannot think of anything else most of the time."

She studied him for a minute. He meant it. He was not marrying her for penance, honor, or to stop gossip. He really wanted to marry her.

"Very well. We can plan the wedding."

He pulled her in for a satisfying, but short kiss since they had arrived at the park.

"One more thing, Hunt," she said.

He kissed her hand. "What is that, my love?"

"When do we break into Melrose's house?"

Hunt dropped his head to his chest and groaned.

16

Diana pulled her black gloves on and stuffed her hair into the black cap she'd borrowed from one of the footmen. She smiled, remembering the argument she'd had with Hunt when she announced she was going with him to search Lord Melrose's house.

"You are not going with me to search Melrose's house, Diana," Hunt had said after she made her intentions known during their carriage ride.

"Why not?"

Hunt squeezed the bridge of his nose. "It's too dangerous, and there is no need for you to involve yourself in this matter."

"I was with you when Lord Melrose spoke with Grafton's footman. In fact, if memory serves, I was the one that brought their conversation to your attention. Therefore, I am already involved."

He gave her a dismissive wave of the hand. "Perhaps that is so, but it is too dangerous." He turned to her. "This is government business that I have been doing for years. Sensitive matters. The fewer people involved the better the outcome."

She sniffed. "Did your contact know that I was the one who discovered the traitorous lord?"

"Yes. It did happen to slip out."

"And?"

"And he didn't seemed pleased, although in all honestly I did not receive the reprimand I expected. Again, I must restate this is too dangerous."

She glared at him. "No more dangerous than it is for you."

"I am a man."

Her brows rose. "And?"

"And I can handle myself in a scuffle." He shook his head. "If I have to worry about your safety, it takes away from my ability to protect myself."

"Hogwash. I know how careful you are about everything, and if you are planning on entering Melrose's house, you have it all worked out." She narrowed her eyes. "Isn't that so?"

He hesitated. "Something could go wrong. No plans are perfect." He glanced to the side and waved to a carriage full of women. Thankfully, the women continued and didn't wave them down. The young girls in the carriage fluttered their eyelashes and twirled their parasols. Hunt ignored them.

He is taken.

Returning to the conversation, she said, "What is the plan?"

"You don't need to know."

"Very well." She raised her chin. "Then I shall wait in my carriage outside your house and follow you wherever you go. I shall probably starve while I await your presence since I dare not leave to eat. People will begin to notice me. Scandal will follow. There will probably be a write-up in the newspaper."

Hunt threw up his hands. "All right. You may go."

"When?"

"I am not certain yet, I'm waiting for word from my valet. He has a contact in Melrose's house who will leave the back door open once they all retire for the night."

"Will that be wise with the chance that Melrose might wander around and find us?"

Hunt shook his head and offered her a look that indicated her comment was precisely why he didn't want her to go with him. "No. I have arranged with my brothers to keep the man at The Rose Room until I send word that I am finished."

"Well done, my lord."

SMIRKING at how she'd gotten Hunt to see things her way, Diana headed down the stairs to the back door to await Hunt's arrival. They'd decided he would leave his carriage parked a block away and meet her at her back door and escort her to the carriage. Even though it was after midnight, there was still a good amount of traffic on the streets with members of the *ton* out and about. They'd decided his carriage parked in front of her house would only start up unnecessary speculation and rumors.

"What the devil are you wearing?" Hunt scowled at her, his hands on his hips.

"Trousers."

"I can see your legs."

She looked down at herself. "Yes, I believe you are correct." She looked up. "Very observant, my lord."

Hunt shook his head and took her arm. "Don't ever wear those in public."

She hurried to keep up with his stride. "Actually, I wear them when I have the opportunity to ride in the country. It's so much more comfortable than balancing in a side-saddle."

"You ride astride?" His voice was so high he squeaked.

"I do. Less dangerous when you take those high jumps."

She wasn't quite sure what he mumbled but most likely she was probably better off not knowing.

He practically tossed her into the carriage, followed her in and slammed the door.

"Really, Hunt, you're tossing me around like I'm some sort of rag doll." She adjusted her shirt and tucked an errant curl into her hat.

"Sorry," he mumbled.

The carriage started their journey and Hunt leaned forward. "You will do exactly as I say when we arrive at Melrose's house. No arguing, suggesting, or going your own way. Agreed?"

She lifted her chin. "That sounds rather tyrannical. I thought we were partners in this."

Hunt leaned forward. "We are not partners. You are here because you wheedled your way in."

"What if I don't agree with those terms?"

He grinned and pulled out a rope from under his seat. "I will tie you up and leave you in the carriage. My driver has instructions to drive around the area with you inside until I come out of the house."

Diana huffed and crossed her arms over her chest. "Despot."

"Just so."

They both grew silent as the carriage came a halt. "Melrose's house is about a block and a half from here. We will walk close to the houses, avoiding the street-lights. With us both dressed in black we should be virtually invisible. Oh, and remember to keep your face pointed toward the buildings."

Diana's heart sped up at what they were about to do. Despite the best plan Hunt had, as he mentioned before, something could always go wrong. What would happen if they were caught? Would they be arrested? Could they end up in jail? She shivered as Hunt held out his hand to assist her from the carriage.

Another benefit to wearing trousers. She really did not need assistance getting into and out of carriages. It was too bad women were banned from wearing such things.

Hunt held her hand as they made their way up the street. He turned them into an alley and made his way up the steps to a back door. He placed his hand on the door latch, turned it and it opened. He pulled her inside.

Diana took a deep breath. This was it.

* * *

HUNT STOPPED ONCE they were inside and the door closed. He had to get his mind off Diana's legs encased so detectably in those trousers and onto the job he needed to perform. He had to find written information that would tie Melrose to the anarchists. Then his job—this assignment—would be finished.

Diana could then plan the wedding, and he would make the arrangements for their wedding trip. Again, his mind drifted to matters other than what they were doing. Bringing Diana along, with her scandalous outfit and familiar scent, was definitely making this assignment more difficult. They needed to search Melrose's library—the most likely place where any papers were stored—and get out.

Marcus's contact had provided Hunt with a rough sketch of the floor where the library was situated. Taking Diana's hand again, he led her up the back stairs to the first floor.

He counted down three doors and then opened the fourth. The library. They entered quietly, and he closed and locked the door. Just in case someone wandered around at night and tried to access the library. They might think it odd that the library was locked, but it would give them time to decide what to do to avoid being caught.

The room was dark, but someone left a small oil lamp lit. Hopefully that was a usual thing to do and any wandering servant would not think it odd to see a bit of light coming from under the door. It was his experience that servants were so well-worked they rarely left their beds once they arrived there.

"You start with the books on the shelves over there." Hunt waved in the general direction of the south wall. "I will go through his desk and also look for a safe where he might have papers."

He breathed a sigh of relief when Diana nodded and walked away from him. She picked up the oil lamp and placed it on the floor where she sat and began to pull books out.

He doubted very much if there were papers hidden in the books, but it was a way to keep Diana in sight and out of trouble while he searched the desk.

He'd brought a small lantern—the same one he used when he searched Mallory's gallery. It wasn't a great deal of light, but with his excellent night vision, he was able to read fairly well.

After about an hour and a half, Hunt pulled out papers from the safe he'd found behind a shelf of books. His training in lock picking paid off again when he was able to get into the safe.

He stared down at the papers, and his lips tightened. Not only was Melrose involved with the anarchists, two MPs were named in a letter Melrose had received.

Hunt folded up the documents and tucked them into his jacket. He closed the safe and straightened up the desk as much as possible, so it didn't look searched.

"Diana," he called in a loud whisper.

"What? I hope you found something since my muscles are getting sore from pulling out books and flipping through them. I must have gone through a hundred books."

"Well, you can stop. I found what I was looking for."

Diana shoved a book back onto the shelf and stood. "Thank goodness. This spying stuff isn't as exciting as I thought it would be."

"Things are rarely as exciting as one thinks they will be." He joined her and placed his hands on her shoulders. "Thank you for your help."

"What help? You found what you were looking for."

His eyes drifted down to her legs. Damn, why did she have to wear those trousers? Slowly he bent his head and brought his mouth to hers. When his tongue nudged her lips, instead of pulling back, she moved closer and opened her mouth.

He wrapped her in his arms and groaned when she shifted, pressing her soft breasts against his chest. No need to wear a corset when one was dressed in trousers. Hunt grasped her chin to tilt her head and take the kiss deeper. Diana was right along with him.

He smiled at her slight moan of disappointment as he pulled back. "We are pushing our luck here, sweetheart. It's best we leave as quickly as possible."

She nodded and took his hand. After he made a quick visual sweep of the room, he opened the door, looked out, and pulled her forward.

They quickly left the house and hurried down the pavement to where the carriage was parked. Hunt helped Diana in and they were off.

Diana looked out the window and frowned. "Where are we going? This is not the way to my house."

"That is correct. I have to stop at The Rose Room and let my brothers know that they can release Melrose now."

Her eyebrows flew to her hairline. "Are they holding him prisoner?"

Hunt laughed. "Not at all. They are just making sure he is enjoying himself enough that he has no interest in leaving."

They arrived at the club within fifteen minutes. Hunt turned to Diana. "I will be right out."

"Wait!" She scuttled forward on her seat. "I want to see the club."

"No," Hunt said. "Women are not allowed. Decent women, that is."

"You mean there are other women in there. Indecent women?"

Hunt leaned back in his seat. Knowing Diana, this would be a longer conversation than he would have liked. "Yes. Women from the demimonde and mistresses are allowed."

"That's not very fair."

"Not so much fair as necessary. Any woman who wants to protect her name would never enter a gambling hell to begin with. Especially since they are not legal."

"If they are illegal, how do you stay open?"

"There are ways that I don't want to go into right now. I am ready to be done with this assignment. Just wait here for a minute, please. I will speak with my brothers and be right back."

Diana opened her mouth to reply, but Hunt hurried off. He shouted back to his driver. "Don't let her out of the carriage."

There was no doubt in his mind that Diana would attempt to sneak into the club, so he needed to make this a fast mission. He sighed, afraid he would spend the rest of his life thwarting Diana's plans to harm herself in some way.

He would have to get her with child post haste to keep her busy at home. Just knowing her as well as he did, Diana would not be one to hand over her child to a nanny and governess to raise. He knew as much as she loved her grandmama, she had missed out on the love and attention of a mother.

Then he smiled at how much pleasure would be gained in the effort to produce his heir.

17

"I don't understand why you think we should invite these gossipmongers to the wedding breakfast. All they will do is criticize us the entire time. It's my wedding, and I want a happy, peaceful event." Diana scowled at Hunt as she scanned the list he'd presented to her of guests to be invited.

They'd already decided on a small ceremony with only Hunt's brothers, a couple of his friends, Diana's father, wife and children, and a few of Diana's friends, one who would act as a bridesmaid. He had wanted to secure a special license, but with Diana's father coming from a distance, his wife had made it known it would be an inconvenience to arrive before a month. So, they had the banns read, instead.

Hunt had cupped her face and rubbed his thumbs over her cheeks. "Sweetheart, we want everyone to know that we are a happy couple, had planned to marry, and are not being forced to do so because of Lord and Lady Grafton's chicanery."

Diana's brows rose. "I see. And having to put up with slurs, suggestions and eye-rolls during our wedding breakfast will assuage their need for nastiness?"

He pulled her into his arms. "Let's just get through this."

She looked up at him. "Just get through this? Isn't every woman entitled to enjoy the day and be pleased with her wedding?" She pulled away from him and rubbed her hands up and down her arms. "Perhaps we should just make the trek to Gretna Green and be done with it. It's already a scandal, so adding to it won't make a bit of difference."

Why she worried about comments and snide remarks was surprising. She'd been dealing with them most of her life. Stunned to feel tears rimming her eyes, she turned her head so Hunt wouldn't notice.

Of course he did.

"Ah, honey, come on. It won't be that bad." He reached for her again and, before she could protest, his mouth covered hers. After a few seconds, her thoughts fled, and she settled into his embrace.

He nudged her tongue, and she opened to him, allowing him to muddle her brain further. Her body reacted just as she'd learned every time Hunt kissed her. Her nipples tingled, and the area between her legs grew moist.

Before she even realized it, he had loosened the back of her gown and had slipped his hand into her corset to fondle her breast. He pulled back and covered her jaw and neck with tiny kisses. "I don't see why we have to wait for the wedding."

She was quite sure she knew to what he was referring, especially given the hardness she felt against her lower abdomen. Hunt was ready to anticipate their vows. Truth be told, so was she, but she suddenly remembered they were standing in her drawing room with an unlocked door.

Good grief, an *open* unlocked door.

Even though she no longer employed a chaperone, any one of the servants could wander by. She shoved him back and pulled up the bodice of her gown. "Hunt, anyone can come in." She barely got the words out, unable to get a full breath.

Hunt ran his fingers through his hair, apparently having a problem breathing also. He grabbed her shoulders and spun her around, quickly lacing up the back of her gown.

Once she was put back together, she hurried to the wall and tugged on the bell pull. "I will order tea."

He walked in the opposite direction. "I could use a brandy."

Two nights later, Diana held onto Hunt's arm as they descended the stairs at the Brentford ball. This one celebrated the come-out of the last of their eight daughters, all who had successfully married and were producing offspring at an alarming rate.

Needless to say, Lord and Lady Brentford appeared a tad desperate.

Lucky for them, however, Lady Alice was a pretty and charming young lady. She'd already attracted a good deal of male attention, but rumor had it she was holding out for a love match. Diana had the feeling if she didn't choose someone by the end of the Season, her father would choose for her.

As usual, she and Hunt attracted attention when they stepped onto the ballroom floor. The room was already filled, with little space to move around and even less to dance.

Diana had to give the Brentfords credit since they had done up the ballroom as splendidly as anyone presenting their first daughter. Flowers filled the room with a lovely scent and footmen were busy carrying trays of champagne.

The refreshment table was loaded with sweet and

savory treats as well as the requisite ratafia, warm lemonade, and punch.

"Why is he not in jail?" Diana nodded toward Lord Melrose as he made his way through the crowd, obviously headed in their direction.

"These things take time," Hunt murmured as Melrose grew closer.

"Good evening, Hunt, Lady Diana." The man bowed to her and slapped Hunt on the back.

"I've been wanting to thank you for arranging for your brothers to extend me further credit." Melrose took time to leer at Diana.

Hunt glared at him. "'Twas no trouble. I hope you made good use of the extension." He grabbed two glasses of champagne from a passing footman and handed one to Diana.

"Well, it seems I'm somewhat in the hole again." Melrose cleared his throat and fiddled with his cravat. "I don't suppose you can speak with them again?"

Knowing Melrose was headed for prison or worse, Hunt had no intention of sticking his brothers—and himself—with additional credits they would never redeem.

"Sorry, old man, but my brothers were tough enough with my last request, so I don't think it would do much good."

Melrose nodded. "I understand. I just know one or more times at the card tables will turn my luck around."

Gamblers always thought the same thing.

Since there didn't seem to be any response to that because Hunt had already told him no, he remained silent. Melrose chatted a bit more and then wandered off.

"Remind me again why he isn't in jail," Diana murmured as they walked toward the edge of the ballroom to stroll.

Hunt was unable to respond since Diana was inundated with requests for dances and Hunt was equally surrounded by eyelash batting young ladies waving their dance cards.

Didn't anyone acknowledge that they were betrothed?

* * *

HUNT STOOD alongside Driscoll at the front of the small church he and Diana had chosen to marry in, instead of one of the larger and better-known ones. With the small group expected to attend, it wouldn't look quite so forlorn for his bride.

His bride.

He still couldn't believe he was marrying Lady Diana Pemberton. Had someone told him that a mere six months ago, he would have laughed himself silly. And then headed out of town.

It had been her idea to have a small ceremony. Also, she would have been happy to only include the few in the church to the wedding breakfast. Despite her argument against it, he knew tongues would continue to wag if they didn't have the lavish wedding breakfast to show the world that Diana was not in the family way, which was among the rumors that had made it to his ears. It was also important for him and Diana to present the picture of a glowingly happy couple not being forced into this marriage.

"Stop fidgeting, Hunt. She'll be here. All brides are late," Driscoll said as he straightened Hunt's cravat.

Hunt slapped his brother's hand away. "I'm not worried. And I don't fidget."

Raised eyebrows was Driscoll's only response. Turning serious, he said, "Are you sure you want to do this, Hunt?"

Hunt scowled. "Don't even think to start that conversation. I am quite happy with my choice of a wife. I might not have anticipated marriage to Diana, but the more I think about it, the smarter my decision seems to be."

"Hardly your decision," Driscoll said as he nodded toward the back of the church. "It appears your bride has arrived."

Diana stood at the back of the church in a white satin gown, that being the chosen color of most brides the last few years. Quite fashionable in style, the sleeves reached her hands, a row of pearls down the center of each sleeve.

The fabric had been pulled back, outlining her stomach and clinging nicely, but modestly, to her breasts. She carried a bouquet of some sort of pink flowers. A white veil that hung almost to the floor covered her head, with a ring of small roses anchoring it to her crown.

Hunt's mouth dried up, and he had one thought, only.

They should skip the wedding breakfast and go right to bed after they chased away the few guests from the church. She raised her head and looked down the aisle. Their eyes met, and Hunt's heartbeat sped up.

"Pull yourself together, man. You're drooling." Driscoll spoke from the side of his mouth.

Hunt straightened and scowled at his brother. "I am not drooling."

She made her way down the aisle on her father's arm. Hunt had met the man for the first time only two days before. Not very impressed with the man, or how he allowed Diana's grandmama to simply whisk her away from him years ago with very little contact over the years, he found it hard to be more than just polite.

Hunt reached out and took her hand when she joined him. "You look beautiful."

"Thank you. I don't mind telling you I am quite

nervous." She took a deep breath, bringing Hunt's eyes right to her breasts.

"Nothing to be worried about, darling. Just another step in life."

She smirked. "More like a leap if you ask me."

The vicar cleared his throat, obviously warning them he was ready to start the ceremony. They turned to him and he began.

"Dearly beloved, we are gathered together here in the sight of God, and in the face of this Congregation, to join together this man and this woman in holy Matrimony; which is an honorable estate, instituted of God in the time of man's innocency—"

Hunt's mind wandered, and he spent his time during the very lengthy introduction to the ceremony thinking about what he was doing. Marriage was forever. Whether Diana turned out to be his perfect mate, or the worst woman he could have ever chosen, it didn't matter.

She was his and would always be his.

He glanced over at her. She seemed to be listening to every word the vicar said. Was she changing her mind? Deciding she didn't want to 'love, honor and obey'? He almost laughed at the 'obey' part. Diana would never obey him. Certainly not like one of the sweet young debutantes he'd first thought would be his choice. He shuddered thinking about standing here with Lady Eunice alongside him.

"I require and charge you both, as ye will answer at the dreadful day of judgement when the secrets of all hearts shall be disclosed, that if either of you know any impediment, why ye may not be lawfully joined together in Matrimony, ye do now confess it—"

Hunt returned to his own thoughts as the vicar droned on, which might have been a bit sacrilegious considering the enormity of what he was undertaking. He really should be paying attention, but he was horrified to realize all his thoughts were now focused on the wedding night.

He was thankful that the wedding breakfast would be held at Diana's house with Lady Greystone, an old friend of her grandmother's, hosting the event there. That way when they were finished eating, he could whisk his new wife off to his townhouse and not have to be concerned with ushering lingering guests out the door.

He managed to pull his attention back as they spoke their vows. Diana's hands were ice cold, and she looked scared to death. "It's all right, sweetheart." He offered her a smile and repeated the vicar's words.

With this Ring I thee wed, with my Body I thee worship, and with all my worldly Goods I thee endow: In the Name of the Father, and of the Son, and of the Holy Ghost. Amen.

He slipped the simple gold band on Diana's finger. Their eyes met, and they both grinned. He knew right then he had made the best decision in his life.

18

With so few people attending the ceremony at the church, it didn't take Diana and her new husband long to sign the marriage register and proceed to their carriage, accepting well wishes from the few attendees along the way.

Even though when planning the wedding she had indicated a small wedding breakfast would be her preference, now she was glad Hunt had insisted on a large one. With the ceremony over, she felt more relaxed and would enjoy a bit of celebration. And food.

Grandmama's fondest friend, Lady Greystone, had offered to oversee the event at Diana's house since Lady Greystone lived in a very small townhouse.

With Diana's father unavailable, Hunt had worked out the marriage contract with Diana's solicitor, and it had been decided she would maintain her townhouse because, with all of Grandmama's things still there, Diana did not have the heart to sell it. She had a few ideas on how to make use of the dwelling. Perhaps a residence for homeless women or neglected children.

She managed to find positions for all her staff either at one of Hunt's properties or with other members of the *ton* for those servants who didn't want to leave London.

"Did I tell you how beautiful you looked?" Hunt sat alongside her in the carriage, holding her hands in his as the carriage began its departure from the church to Diana's townhouse.

"Yes. I believe you did." She smirked at him. "You look quite the dandy yourself, my lord."

Hunt placed his palm on her cheek. "You know that tiny little kiss the vicar allowed at the end of the ceremony was hardly enough time for a decent one with my new wife."

Oh, dear. All of a sudden, the air in the carriage seemed to disappear, and heat settled in her middle. "Yes. Hardly enough time." Was that her voice panting like that?

Without further conversation, Hunt lowered his head and took her mouth in a kiss that could only be called possessive. Different from their prior kisses. Someone made a slight growl. She thought it was Hunt, but with how she was responding to his kiss, it could very well have been her.

He pulled her close, and she slid her hands up his chest to encircle his neck. Their tongues dueled for possession and control. Of course, Hunt being the more experienced one, he won the physical debate.

Not that she minded. She was having too good of a time.

All too soon, it seemed, he pulled back and cupped her face, rubbing his thumbs over her cheeks. "We are going to have a good marriage, Diana. I promise you."

"I hope so. I know I wasn't your ch—"

"Stop." He closed his eyes and shook his head. "I don't want to hear that again. You *were* my choice. I am not arrogant enough to think you believe it started out that way, but I assure you *nothing*, and absolutely *no one*, forced me to speak those vows today. I want you, and I know we will suit quite well."

"I will try to be a good wife, Hunt. Honest. I know I've had my stumbles, but I am looking forward to what all young ladies look towards. My own home, a husband, children. . ."

The rakish glimmer in his eyes brought back the fluttering in her middle. "Yes, dear wife. Let's talk about the making of children." He smiled and pulled her back toward him as the carriage came to a rolling stop in front of her townhouse.

"Ah, too late."

The extra grooms and footmen they hired for the day were busy helping the guests from their carriages and moving the vehicles to the mews.

Hunt climbed out of the carriage and turned to assist her. "Ready, sweetheart?"

Diana took a deep breath. "As ready as I ever will be."

They entered the house and were immediately surrounded by guests. Lady Greystone directed the footmen to assist in forming a line so the guests could greet the bridal couple.

The air-kissing, bowing and curtseying seemed to take forever and, by the time all the guests made their way through the line, Diana was parched, her feet hurt, and she was ready to eat. Being a bit nervous, she had skipped her usual toast and hot chocolate that morning.

"Are you feeling all right, sweeting? You look a bit worn."

"I am. I'd like nothing more than to sit down and have a cup of tea."

"So it shall be." Hunt waved one of the footmen over. "Please have tea sent to Lady Huntington's place at the table."

Lady Huntington.

Diana started at those words. That was now her. She was no longer Lady Diana Pemberton. She had a new title, a new name, a new residence. And a new husband, who apparently was quite solicitous.

A good start.

"Come." He took her hand and walked her away from the line.

"What about the guests who haven't arrived yet?"

"They can greet us when they arrive. You need to sit down and have some tea." He regarded her. "I'll bet you skipped your breakfast this morning, did you not?"

She smiled at his concern. "This is our breakfast, remember?"

"Ah. Well done, my lady. However, a bit of tea will calm you down." He walked them both to the table where the bride and groom were to sit. Driscoll already sat in his seat, with Dante alongside him. Next to Diana's seat was Patricia McDowell, her best friend from school.

Even though they had only seen each other a couple times since Patricia married a Highlander, she still made the trip to London to act as bridesmaid. Her Highlander husband was so big he terrified Diana when she first met him at Patricia's wedding.

However, from what Patricia had told her and what she'd witnessed herself, Laird Ashton was besotted with his wife and three small daughters. Patricia also assured Diana that he was so thrilled with the little girls he had no cares that there were no sons. So far, Patricia had added, as she'd giggled and blushed. Which left Diana thinking her friend was in a family way again.

Diana stopped briefly at the table where her father and his family sat to have a few words with them. They were going to spend some time at Diana's townhouse and see the London sights before heading back to their home in South Yorkshire.

Before Diana had taken even one sip of her tea, the

footmen began serving the breakfast Diana had planned with Cook. Marinated South Uist salmon, Lyme Bay crab, Hebridean langoustines over an herb salad, Highland Mey Select lamb, Highland Grove spring vegetables, English Asparagus, Jersey potatoes, sauce Windsor, and a trio of Berkshire honey ice cream, sherry trifle and chocolate parfait for dessert, along with the beautiful wedding cake that had been placed in the center of the table where Diana, Hunt, Driscoll and Patricia sat.

Diana was quite pleased at how well the food looked and tasted. Cook was definitely due a boon for the fine meal she had prepared.

* * *

AS FINE A MEAL as Diana's staff had cooked and served, Hunt was anxious to finish up the feast and hustle his bride out of the house and to his townhouse.

He'd had his staff prepare his bedchamber with flowers and champagne and warned them that he and his bride would not be leaving the room until the next morning, so dinner and the following morning's breakfast was to be served in the bedchamber.

Since he had duties to perform in Parliament, he could only squeak out a week to take Diana on a wedding trip. Diana had confessed to him at one time that she loved the city of Bath, so Hunt had arranged for them to stay in the Gainsborough Bath Spa. Named after the famous and beloved painter, Sir Thomas Gainsborough, the hotel was centered around Spa Village Bath and had the exclusive privilege of direct access to the natural thermal, mineral-rich waters, for which the city was famous.

Diana had assured him her bags were packed, and Driscoll would see them to the train in the morning. He sighed. Would the wedding breakfast ever be over?

"What's wrong?" Diana asked as she viewed him over the rim of her wine glass. "You keep sighing."

"Nothing, my pet." He leaned in, close to her ear. "I am merely anxious to get you alone."

Heat rose to her face, and she glanced around. "Shh, Hunt. People might hear you."

Hunt's eyebrows rose. "And you think anyone here, within, or not within, hearing distance would be surprised to hear me say that?"

"I'm not surprised," Driscoll chimed in. He grinned at Diana and raised his glass in a salute. "In fact, I will give a toast now, brother, so you can easily use that as an excuse to slip away."

"But we haven't cut the wedding cake yet." Diana eyed the beautiful monstrosity of three layers, decorated with pink and yellow flowers. "Cook did such a splendid job on it."

"Very well, then," Driscoll said. "I shall make a toast to your happiness and upcoming offspring production—"

Diana sucked in a deep breath. "Don't you dare, Driscoll, or my first job as your sister-in-law would be to throttle you."

"Nonsense, Diana, dear. You would not wish to get blood on that lovely gown."

"Leave her alone, Driscoll," Hunt growled.

Diana was pleased by Hunt's remark and Driscoll's surprised expression. After so many years of only having her grandmama as a champion, she now had Hunt.

Although truth be told, she'd always had Hunt. Wasn't he the one she constantly turned to when in trouble?

Driscoll called a footman over and gave instructions to have everyone served champagne. While that was being done, Diana and Hunt cut the cake which was then taken to the kitchen to be sliced into individual pieces for the guests.

Her brother-in-law stood and held up his glass. "I would like to take this opportunity to congratulate my brother on his excellent choice of a bride and wish them all the happiness in the world."

Cheers resounded and everyone took a sip. "And," he continued, looking down at Diana and Hunt, "may your '*for better or worse*' be a lot better than worse." He smiled at Diana. "Welcome to the family, Lady Huntington."

19

Hunt entered his bedchamber after a quick bath to see Diana standing in front of the fireplace in a white silk dressing gown with her pink toes peeking out from below the nightgown underneath. Her hair was loose and falling around her shoulders, the curls reaching almost to her waist.

A slight blush rose to her face as she twisted her fingers, an uneasy smile on her plump, rose-colored lips. It appeared his bold and brave wife had lost some of her audaciousness.

He, on the other hand, was without air. Diana was stunning. He'd bedded many women in his life, some with amazing skill and seductive powers, but none had ever affected him the way his innocent bride did. As much as he wanted and desired her, he was overcome with the need to take her in his arms and tell her there was nothing to be afraid of.

"You look lovely, sweetheart." He moved closer to her, and she took one step back. He reached his hand out. "Come here."

If they were to have a pleasurable night, one worthy of his bride, he would have to calm whatever concerns she had. "Let's have a glass of champagne."

Her shoulders relaxed, and her nervous smile turned genuine. "That's a splendid idea."

He walked to the small table underneath the window where the bottle he'd ordered sat and poured two glasses. He returned to the two comfortable chairs in front of the fireplace and handed her one.

He took his seat and leaned back, resting his foot on his knee, careful to keep his dressing gown closed lest his bride jump up and race from the room. "Did you enjoy the wedding breakfast?" It was best to start with something innocuous to relax her.

"Yes. In fact, I must tell you that I am glad you did not go along with my initial wishes and have a small celebration. It was nice to see my father and his family, even though Lady Rockingham and I had never been more than passing acquaintances."

"She seems like a pleasant woman." Hunt viewed her over the rim of his glass, noting that his wife's color had returned to normal and she seemed less anxious.

"I guess so." She shrugged. "I was whipped away from my father's home by Grandmama before I even got to know the woman. It did always trouble me, however, that Papa married his wife before a full year of mourning was up. During that time, he and I became close, but once his new wife appeared, things changed, then Grandmama arrived and off I went."

She shifted in her chair to face him directly. "Your brothers are looking good. Since they spend so much time at the club, I never see them. They don't move about in Society, do they?"

Hunt shook his head as he refilled their glasses. "No. Driscoll was always too serious for the frivolity of the *ton*, and Dante, even though fully accepted by our father and raised with us, was never comfortable with Society."

"I imagine with their good looks they would both be easily accepted."

"Ah, so my bride notices my brothers' good looks. Didn't you know you are supposed to only admire me?" He downed the last of his drink and placed the glass on the small table between them, ready to move the evening's activities along. He patted his thighs. "Come sit on my lap."

Diana smirked. "Becoming anxious, my lord?" Her nervousness seemed to have passed. The wine had done its job.

She stood, took the last sip from her glass, and placed it next to his. After crossing the space between them, she sat on his lap, wrapping her arms around his neck.

"So sweet." Hunt dipped his head and took her lips in a soft, nibbling kiss. Once she pressed harder against his mouth, he pulled her flush to his body and turned the kiss into something erotic and possessive.

Flower-scented locks from her head fell to surround them like a curtain. He nudged her lips to open and then swept in, tasting, feeling, plundering. She met him touch for touch, a slight moan coming from somewhere deep inside her.

Hunt ran his hands up her curves to her shoulders and slipped the dressing gown off. It pooled in her lap. He pulled back and ran the backs of his fingers down her cheek. "We will be more comfortable in the bed."

She shook her head. "Not yet." Leaning forward, she kissed his jaw and licked the sensitive skin under his ear.

He felt her smile against his skin when he moaned. Taking back control, he cupped her face and covered her mouth with a long, slow, sultry kiss. Diana began to shift on his lap which, given the size of his erection, was not a good idea.

"Easy, darling." To get her into the bed, he had to raise her passion that he tasted before to match his.

With a flick of his wrists, he brushed the thin straps

holding up her silk nightgown. It slithered down her body, teasing him, revealing the most beautiful sight he'd ever seen. Full, rounded breasts with dusky nipples, pert and already hard as pebbles. He could not stop staring. "Oh, sweetheart," he breathed.

He covered her shoulders with his hands and tilted her body back. Placing his lips on her breast, he licked a nipple and then covered the entire area with his mouth and suckled as greedily as a babe.

Diana grabbed the sides of his head with her hands, digging her fingernails into his scalp, and moaned.

"Does that feel good?"

"Yes. Yes. It does." Her voice was breathless, her panting filling the air with the sounds of pleasure.

It was time to relocate to the more comfortable bed. "Stand up, sweeting," he mumbled not taking his mouth from her breast.

"Can't."

Hunt pulled back and placed his hands under her arms and lifted her to her feet. The dressing gown and nightgown slid to the floor in a rush of silk. He sat back, and she stood before him, the firelight accenting her curves. "My God, Diana. You're stunning." His eyes never leaving her, moving over her glorious form, he shook his head. "Mallory got it all wrong."

She sucked in a breath and, as much as he wanted to have her just stand there so he could admire the breathtaking beauty she was, her reaction to his comment warned him the blackguard was not a subject they should discuss. To distract her, he stood and scooped her into his arms, kicking her garments aside as he kissed her, and moved them to the bed.

* * *

HUNT LAID her gently on top of the counterpane. It was cool on her back after the warmth of the fireplace and Hunt's kisses and caresses.

Diana smiled up at him as he rested one knee on the bed alongside her. "Am I to be the only one undressed, then?" She felt the slight blush from before returning to crawl up her body to her face.

"Not at all." He untied the belt of his dressing gown and shrugged out of the garment. Her mouth dried up as her eyes wandered down his impressive, muscular body and landed on the very strong evidence of his desire.

She swallowed. "Um, do you think this is going to work?" She looked up to catch him swallowing a smile.

"Yes, my love, this will work. Have no fear. The good Lord knew what he was doing."

Realizing that she was lying naked as the day she was born, stretched out on the bed while Hunt looked at her as if she was his next meal, she scooted over and pulled part of the counterpane over her.

"No, my sweet. No need to cover yourself."

She blushed. "I'm cold."

He pulled back the covers and joined her on the bed, causing her to edge farther back. "I have a remedy for that. A very satisfying, pleasurable remedy." Reaching out, he took her hand and tugged her forward.

The fluttering inside her stomach increased as he moved her closer to him, and their hungry mouths met, Hunt's warm body covering hers. His hand rubbed her shoulders gently, then made their way down her back to cup her derrière. "So soft, your skin is like silk."

With his arm wrapped around her bottom, he shifted them so they were facing each other, laying side by side on the bed. He gently fingered a lock of her hair, sniffing it, then running it over his lips. "I want to take our time. We have all night."

She, on the other hand, wanted to move things

along. Grandmama had told her about a woman's first time joining with a man, but even though she tried to make it sound wonderful, to Diana, it had all sounded very messy and painful.

"Stop thinking." Hunt moved his hand up to cup her breast and run his thumb over her nipple. Diana closed her eyes as the wonderful sensation raced through her. Not wanting to just lie there like a lump of clay, she kissed the hollow of his neck, then moved her mouth down to playfully lick his flat dark nipple.

Hunt drew in a breath.

"Does that feel good?"

"Yes." He rolled over her and once more covered her breast with his warm, moist mouth. Her legs grew restless and, like it had the few times they kissed, the area between her legs felt swollen and damp. "Please."

"What, my love?" He nibbled on her collarbone, his warm breath raising small bumps on her skin.

"I need more." She barely got the words out.

Almost as an apology, he murmured, "Ah, of course you do." He continued to taunt her nipples with his tongue as his hand skimmed down her body, increasing the tension in her middle.

Eventually, his fingers slid between her legs, and she immediately felt the need for release grow. "Please, Hunt."

His thumb circled a small nubbin at the opening to her core. She sucked in a deep breath as her muscles grew tighter. He kept it up for a few minutes while kissing her, murmuring words she didn't even understand in her ear until she couldn't stand it anymore. "Harder."

Hunt returned to her breast to tease it once more as his fingers worked frantically to bring her release. His thumb continued to circle the piece of flesh while his finger slid into her opening.

Her body bucked as she threw her head back and

called his name, over and over. "Yes. Please. Yes. Don't stop."

"Oh, I won't sweetheart. Take your time, I will be here to catch you."

Waves of pleasure washed over her as she pressed hard against Hunt's hand, and the throbbing continued. With a deep breath, she collapsed onto the bed, a soft smile on her face.

Grandmama was correct.

"I loved watching you," Hunt said as he continued to play with the area between her legs. He pushed a second finger into her opening. "You are so warm, tight, and wet."

Diana panted her words. "I assume that's good?"

"Oh, yes, my love. Very, very good."

Feeling daring, Diana reached down and cupped Hunt's throbbing member. It felt strange. Steel covered with satin. She squeezed, and he grunted.

She pulled her hand back. "Does that hurt?"

"No." The word came out as a groan. "It feels wonderful, but it's bringing me closer."

She knew from Grandmama's conversations that he meant it was time for him to insert himself into her body. She did not believe for one minute it was going to be an easy job for him to do. He was so large.

She took a deep breath, stiffened her body, fisted her hands by her side, pinched her eyes closed and said, "I'm ready."

After a few seconds, Hunt burst out laughing. "Oh, my love, you were very, very ready a little bit ago, but now you look as though you are waiting for the executioner."

He returned to her mouth and began the process all over again. Kissing, nipping, sucking, nibbling, until she couldn't think straight. Her body relaxed, and she felt the build up once again between her legs. Just as the thought crossed her mind that now was a good time for

Hunt to try the impossible, he spread her legs wide and began to edge his way inside. "Relax, sweetheart. Stop thinking."

She opened her mouth to respond just as he thrust forward. A slight pinch caused her to cry out, but otherwise, she only felt full. Hunt remained still and brushed the hair from her forehead. "Are you well?"

Diana squeezed her inner muscles, and Hunt groaned again. "Yes, I think I am well."

"Thank God." He slid back out and then in again, eventually developing a rhythm that she followed.

"Wrap your legs around me," he said right before he took her mouth in a kiss that brought on another wave of pleasure just as Hunt gave one final push and moaned her name.

She could feel the warmth from his seed entering her as she again sunk into a heap.

Her body was slick with sweat, and she had a devil of a time breathing. After a few minutes, Hunt rolled onto his back and pulled her against him. "I will get up to help you clean up. I just need a minute." Their combined pants filled the room, along with the scent of love-making.

After her heartbeat slowed and they had both regained their breath, Hunt turned to her, pushing the damp strands of hair from her forehead. "Wife of mine, I must say I have never before laughed in the middle of sexual activity."

She looked up at him and frowned. "Is that good or bad?"

20

Hunt smiled down at his wife as the carriage left the Gainsborough Bath Spa to take them to the train station for their trip back to London. They'd spent a full week partaking of the waters, strolling the charming town, eating at various and well-known restaurants, visiting museums and theaters, and best of all, making love a few times a day.

He'd found Diana to be all that he wanted and needed in a wife. She was witty in a derisive sort of way, intelligent in her curiosity about the places they'd visited and new things they'd seen, caring and loving enough to be a wonderful mother, and passionate in the bedchamber.

Perhaps she'd given him cause for concern in the past with her antics, but he'd seen a new level of maturity in her since her return from Italy. Even the scandals that had driven him to sneak into Mallory's studio, and their quick betrothal and marriage, had not been her fault.

Yes, life would be pleasant with her at his side.

"Did you have a nice visit?" He brushed a loose curl behind her ear.

"Yes. It was lovely. I hope we can travel to Italy some

time so I can show you all the interesting and noteworthy things there. Especially Rome. You would love seeing the coliseum."

"We will. I promise to take you there before our first child is born."

Diana grinned. "Um, the way we carried on this last week that child might not be too far in the future."

He raised her hand and kissed her knuckles. "It's a promise. Things will be much better once this session of Parliament adjourns. I will work on getting estate matters taken care of as well so we can spend a few weeks in Italy."

Shortly afterwards, they left the carriage and entered the train depot. The station was busy, porters running back and forth with luggage, and the conductors helping passengers settle into the cars. They had first-class reservations, which included the dining service, so they could break their fast on their way home.

They spent the time discussing the things they did and then switched to how Diana wanted to redecorate his townhouse. "I will be happy to use my inheritance from Grandmama and the sale of her manor next to your family estate that you so graciously allowed me to keep in my own name for the expenses."

Hunt wiped his mouth with his napkin and placed it alongside his plate. "Not necessary, sweetheart. I want that money to stay for your and our children's benefit. I have enough money to cover whatever you wish to do in London or at my country estate. Remember, as your husband, it is my duty to provide for your food, clothing, and shelter."

"No matter how elaborate I need that shelter to be?" She smirked.

"I trust you."

A few minutes of comfortable silence passed, then

Diana said, "I need to decide what I will do with my townhouse in London."

He leaned back in the seat and crossed his arms. "Do you have any ideas?"

She placed her teacup in the saucer and looked out the window at the passing scenery. "I have been considering turning it into a home for abandoned children, or possibly women who have no home."

"Quite noble of you, my dear. Have you considered how to maintain the dwelling? You will need sponsors, I would think, unless you wish to use your inheritance for that purpose."

"I am giving that some thought. As I said, it's just some ideas I've had."

The trip passed quickly and soon they were off the train and, after using a hackney, they rolled to a stop in front of the townhouse.

"I feel odd walking up the steps knowing this is my home now," Diana said as she took his arm, and they made their way to the front door.

"You will feel more at home once you see your belongings here."

"My things should have been moved while we were away, and Marguerite will have found room—I hope—for my wardrobe." She grinned at her husband. "It is quite extensive, you know."

He patted her hand. "That is no problem. We will find room for everything. And remember, once Parliament ends and we move to my estate, you may take as many rooms as you like to fill with your clothing."

Diana huffed. "I don't have *that* much."

During one of the many discussions they'd had during their wedding trip, Hunt had made it known to his wife that, although she had her own chamber next to the sitting room joining their bedchambers at the townhouse and estate, he would prefer they slept together.

As he'd pointed out to her, most times, once they made love, they were both too exhausted to move anyway and, since his bed was bigger and more comfortable, his room it would be. Now that he'd gotten her into his bed, he planned to keep her there all night.

The red door with the quaint knocker opened, and they were greeted by Peters. Seeing the man's rough-hewn face reminded Hunt that he needed to explain the man to Diana, as well as his valet, Marcus, since given their rough background, she would not understand occasional slips of the tongue.

Although she knew several of the staff from her occasional visits to his home, Hunt decided a formal introduction to the small number of servants as they lined up in the entrance hall to greet them was appropriate.

As expected, Diana was gracious and charming to the staff. She spoke with each one, asking their names and inquiring about their families. It was apparent to him from their beaming faces that they loved their new mistress already.

His housekeeper, Mrs. Grady, stepped forward once the introductions were complete. "My lady, I am at your service whenever you wish to tour the house and go over the household accounts. Cook is waiting to meet with you also to go over the menu."

Diana dipped her head. "Thank you so much, Mrs. Grady, but I think for today I will just trust whatever Cook has planned for the day. May we meet first thing in the morning for the tour?"

"Yes. That is perfect. Now may we prepare tea for you and his lordship?"

Diana turned to him. "Tea?"

"No. I think not. I have work to catch up on, and I'm still full from our breakfast, but you go ahead if you wish."

"I think not, Mrs. Grady. Like his lordship, I am still full from breakfast."

She curtsied. "Very well, then. Luncheon will be at one o'clock."

Hunt gave her a quick kiss on the cheek and took her hand again. "I will let you check on your maid and see you at luncheon." He turned on his heel, feeling quite happy, and strode to the library.

* * *

DIANA PADDED up the carpeted stairs to Hunt's bedchamber. Although she would sleep there, she had decided to store most of her belongings from her London townhouse in the room connected to the sitting room between them. Then, when they moved to the country estate, most of it would go there since that was much larger than this house.

"My lady, how lovely to see you. Did you have a nice trip?" Marguerite greeted her as she entered the room, taking items out of a trunk. There were still barrels and boxes of clothing scattered around the room.

"It was lovely. Again, I'm sorry you didn't go with us."

Marguerite waved her off. "That's fine, my lady. I'm not one for travel, anyway." She blushed slightly. "Although I must say it was quite titillating to know your husband wanted to be your lady's maid."

Diana blushed along with her. She'd been surprised when Hunt told her that he was very adept at dressing and undressing women, so they didn't need a third person on their honeymoon. He'd left his valet in London, also. The entire time they were gone, Diana had kept her hair in a simple style that she could do herself. She grinned, remembering some of the undressing sessions they'd had.

Diana turned in a circle, her hands on her hips. "Where are we going to put all of this?"

Marguerite nodded toward a wardrobe against the wall. "I was able to clear out some space in that one." She continued to pull out gowns and shake them.

Diana walked over to the wardrobe. Sitting alongside it was a picture frame with a piece of linen draped over it. The closer she got, the more anxious she became, her heart pounding and her mouth dry. It looked familiar and, with a shaky hand, she pulled up the fabric and gasped.

"Is something wrong, my lady?" Marguerite asked.

Diana was staring at the portrait Hunt was supposed to burn. Her thoughts were so muddled she couldn't speak. He'd kept it all this time! Had he spent his nights ogling her?

She growled and flipped the linen down, picked up the vile painting, and marched across the room. "I will be back, Marguerite."

Or not.

She flew down the stairs, almost losing her footing as she rounded the corner and headed toward the library. She flung the door open to see Hunt sitting at his desk. He looked up and smiled. Within seconds, his smile dimmed. "Is something wrong, sweetheart?"

Diana stormed up to the desk and slammed the painting in front of him, then came within inches of his face. "Don't you sweetheart me. You, you, you blackguard!" She quelled the urge to slap his face. How dare he keep that horrible portrait right here in his house where anyone who spotted it could lift the linen and look at it.

She was mortified.

He looked down, his face growing pale. "The portrait?"

"Yes. The. . .the, portrait! I see by your reaction you know exactly what I'm talking about." She stamped her foot, feeling quite foolish, but uncaring how juvenile it looked. "You promised you would burn it!"

"Now wait a minute, Diana. I did not promise I would burn it. You asked me to, but I have been yet unable to do so."

She crossed her arms under her breasts and tapped her foot. Oh, the man was impossible. She lowered her voice, trying hard to be an adult about this. "In *all this time*, you haven't been able to burn it?"

He stood and threw out his hands. "Do you have any idea what the smell of burning paint would be like?"

She shook her head.

"Well, neither do I. But I'm sure it's not pleasant and would encourage questions."

She dropped her arms to the side. "I can't trust you." She stared at him. "I Can't. Trust. You. How can we have a marriage if there is no trust?"

Hunt ran his fingers through his hair. "You are taking this too far. Of course you can trust me. I'm your husband."

Diana backed away. "No. I cannot trust you. You knew how important this was to me. You were to steal the portrait and then burn it. Marguerite moved it out of a wardrobe in my bedchamber to make room for my clothes. Anyone coming into the room, for any reason, could look at it."

He just shook his head.

"I. . . I have to leave." She turned. "I must go."

"Diana, wait!"

She hurried away, tears stinging her eyes. She raced up the stairs, went into the bedchamber where Marguerite still worked, and said, "Get your coat. We are leaving."

Her eyes wide, Marguerite must have seen something in her face because she never questioned her but merely dropped the gown she was shaking out, grabbed her coat, and followed Diana down the steps.

"May I have the carriage brought around, my lady?" Peters asked as they arrived at the door.

"No, but thank you. We will hire a hackney." She grabbed Marguerite's hand and dragged her out the door, down the steps, and practically ran them both down the pavement until they reached an empty hackney. She gave the address of her townhouse, climbed inside, and leaned her head against the squab.

"I believe I have made a huge mistake." With those words, she covered her face with her hands and burst into tears.

21

Hunt collapsed into his chair and rubbed his eyes with his thumb and index finger. What a mess. The blasted portrait would be the death of him. Truth be told, after the first couple of days after he stole it, still wondering how he was going to burn it without raising questions, he had forgotten about the damn thing. He shoved it into the wardrobe in Diana's bedchamber and wiped it from his mind.

Now it was back to haunt him once more. She thought she couldn't trust him. Well, she had good reason.

Peters slowly approached the desk. "This just came for you, my lord." He held out a salver with a letter sitting on top. "Is everything all right, my lord? Her ladyship seemed to be in quite a hurry to leave."

Hunt took the envelope, broke the seal, and read the summons from Sir Phillip. He dropped it on the desk. "No. Everything is not all right." He leaned back in his chair and stared at the ceiling.

After a perfectly wonderful wedding trip where he'd been looking forward to a strong, happy marriage with Diana, his stupid decision to not get rid of the portrait immediately could very well wipe it all out.

"Can I do anything to help?" Peters asked.

"Yes. You can." Hunt banged his fist on the painting. "Get rid of this. Take it somewhere you can burn it and not raise suspicion."

Peter's eyebrows rose to his hairline. "Burn it, my lord?"

"Burn it. Wherever you take it, make sure you stay right there until nothing is left but ashes." He stood and grabbed his jacket from the chair where he'd dropped it when he entered the room. "I'm leaving."

He was so angry he felt as though he should walk to Sir Phillip's well-disguised office just to get himself under control. However, it would take him a good two hours to do so, and he had no idea how important the summons was. Instead, he strode to the mews and waited impatiently as the groom readied his horse.

What had Diana meant when she left? Was she merely going out for the afternoon to calm herself down? Did she plan on leaving him permanently? All her belongings were still at his house.

He sighed as he swung his leg over Black Diamond and made his way to the street.

His thoughts were still muddled by the time he reached Sir Phillip's office. Hunt took the steps two at a time and dropped the knocker on the door. Sir Phillip himself answered and waved Hunt in. "Come in, come in. I wasn't sure if you had returned from your wedding trip."

Most likely Sir Phillip knew precisely which train they'd arrived on, where they'd been, how long they'd stayed, and which restaurants, theaters, and museums they'd visited.

The man knew everything.

Once they were settled in the room the size of a large closet, Sir Phillip rested his folded hands on his desk and regarded him. "I wanted to advise you of the status on the Melrose matter."

Hunt nodded.

"Melrose was picked up by Scotland Yard—at the Home Office's behest--and was turned over to me. After a lengthy conversation, he cleared up a few matters."

"What is that?"

"Melrose was not in as deep as we thought. However, he did provide us with names that we are pursuing. The main lead he offered was the name of the man who killed Mallory and then burned his gallery down. The idiot hoped Mallory's body would be unrecognizable and Scotland Yard would not discover he'd been shot first."

Hunt shook his head. "So the investigation is over? Or continues? And what happens to Melrose? He is still a peer involved with an anarchist group."

"Lord Melrose left for America while you were romancing your new wife in Bath. The investigation continues but, at this point, there is nothing that requires your particular skills."

Sir Phillip stood and offered his hand. "Congratulations on your marriage, my lord. I wish you many years of happiness."

Hunt rose and took the man's hand. They remained silent as Sir Phillip walked him to the door. He stepped out into the gloomy day and made his way to the mews to retrieve Black Diamond.

I wish you many years of happiness.

TWO DAYS PASSED with no word from Diana. He noticed when he entered the library the morning after his meeting with Sir Phillip that the painting was gone from his desk.

Good riddance.

No one from his staff mentioned Diana's absence, which told him they knew something was wrong.

Marcus, of course, voiced his unrequested opinion of young wives fleeing their husbands, but Hunt knew in his heart it was all his fault.

He also came to the realization that he was madly in love with Diana, had probably been most of his life, and would do whatever it took to get her back. Perhaps a visit to The Rose Room might distract him. He could have a few drinks, antagonize his brothers, and forget everything for a while.

He'd gone to Diana's house twice but was told both times she was not at home. Whether that was true, or she was refusing to see him, he had no idea, but he must come up with a plan. Diana was his, and he would get her back.

As usual, instead of going to the front door of The Rose Room, Hunt entered through the back door and took the stairs to the office floor. From the sound of voices coming from the game floor, business was doing well.

"Well, the happily married man has returned from his honeymoon. I would think you had more interesting things to do than bother us." Dante leaned back on his chair, with his feet on the desk. Hunt swiped at his boots and asked his usual question. "Why aren't you working?"

"I'm on a break," Dante and Hunt said at the same time, then grinned at each other.

Driscoll had his head bent over his books and ignored the brothers.

Still feeling restless, Hunt said, "I'm going downstairs. At least someone should oversee the business."

He left to the sound of Dante's laughter. As he entered the gaming room, it was just as he'd expected. Busy, noisy and crowded. Hunt went to the bar and ordered a brandy. He took a sip and turned to survey the area. As he observed the activity, his eyes wandered the room, noting the solid crowd and raucous conversation and excitement that was generally found in the club. Taking another sip, his eyes settled on a new addition on the east wall.

He squinted at the spot and, with a sense of horror, he carefully placed his partially empty glass on the bar and walked slowly past the gamers, barely acknowledging calls and comments from friends. The closer he drew to the wall, the harder his blood pumped through his body, until he thought his head would explode.

There in plain sight, hanging on the wall in the gaming room of the well-populated, well-known Rose Room, was Diana's portrait.

* * *

Diana sat, staring out the window at the dark, misty night, her chin resting on her propped-up hand. She sighed. What a mess this had become. As much as she hated to admit it, she missed the cad.

She'd realized with the portrait sitting in that wardrobe, there was little chance of anyone seeing it. But she still had relied on him destroying the thing. Did that mean she could never trust him?

Lud, hadn't she been hurt and embarrassed herself when she'd been judged on all the things she'd botched up? Especially since Hunt was the one who usually pulled her feet from the fire. Should she judge him the same way?

She finally admitted she was in love with her dastardly husband and really didn't want the marriage to end with them separated. Once they put this behind them, they could have a good marriage. And children. She would love children.

With a sense of relief, and excited for the first time in days, she scooted from the chair, her mind made up. She would go to Hunt's townhouse—*their* townhouse—

and settle the matter. She grinned. Of course, she would have him grovel first.

She raced upstairs and changed into one of the few gowns that had been left behind when Marguerite had arranged for her clothes to be moved. It was outdated but still fashionable. "Marguerite!"

The maid entered the room, a smirk on her face. "Going somewhere, my lady?"

"Yes!" She turned her back. "Will you please fasten me up and see what you can do with my hair?"

"Will you need me to accompany you?" Marguerite quickly fastened the gown and pointed to the chair in front of the dressing table. "Let's see how we can make something lovely out of this mess."

Diana laughed. "That's exactly what I propose to do. Make something lovely out of a mess." At the time the portrait had been stolen, she'd told Marguerite all about it and how Hunt was to burn the thing. Instead of being outraged on her mistress's account when they'd discovered the painting in the wardrobe, Marguerite viewed him not burning the portrait as amusing. Her words: "This could very well be what led Lord Huntington to propose."

At which time Diana reminded her maid that there was no 'proposal', just an avoidance of scandal.

"There. You look lovely. Shall I send for the carriage?"

Diana stood and pulled on her gloves. "Yes, please. I will be down in a few minutes."

Marguerite left the room, and Diana placed her hands on her stomach and took a deep breath. Yes, this was the right thing to do. Briggs had told her that Hunt had called twice when she was out. She wondered if her husband believed she was truly out or if she was hiding from him.

She picked up her reticule and left the room. Briggs awaited her at the door, holding her short pelisse which she shrugged into. She fastened up the buttons, her hands shaky and her mouth dry. This was silly, and she must pull herself together. But she could not deny the excitement she felt at seeing Hunt again.

Blast the man.

The carriage ride was short, and her stomach was in knots by the time they arrived. Peters had the door opened before she reached the top step. "I am sorry, my lady, but his lordship is out for the evening."

"Oh." Her sense of excitement crumbled. "Did he say where he was going, or when he would return?"

"I believe he was visiting his brothers at The Rose Room. If you would like to come in and wait, I can have tea sent in."

She glided past Peters and entered the drawing room. "Yes, that would be good." She began to slide her gloves off when she called, "Peters."

"Yes, my lady." He hadn't gone far.

"No need for tea. I will be leaving."

His shoulders slumped. "Oh, my lady. I believe his lordship really wanted to speak with you."

She grinned and headed back to the door. "And that is precisely what he is going to do." She sailed past him, down the steps, and back to her carriage. "The Rose Room, please, John."

Like most women of her station, she had always wondered what the inside of the most exclusive and popular gaming hell was like. The business kept a low profile since gambling was illegal, but because most of the people who made the laws and could enforce the law visited on a regular basis, the Rose brothers were seldom bothered by raids.

Once they rolled up to the front door, she decided going around back might be a better idea. Hunt had told her more than once that the only women who patronized the club were mistresses and the demimonde. She still planned to go inside to see him, but she didn't want to flaunt herself by using the front door. After all, she was here to make up with her husband, not antagonize him.

The man at the back door admitted her when she identified herself. He gave her directions on how to reach the business offices which were where she planned to start her search for Hunt.

Driscoll sat at his desk, hovering over a book of numbers. There was no sign of either Dante or Hunt.

"Is Hunt here, Driscoll?"

The man jumped, apparently so enamored of his numbers that he hadn't heard her enter. "Oh, Diana, you startled me." He frowned. "What are you doing here? Women aren't allowed. At least not decent women."

"I'm looking for Hunt. His butler thought he was here."

"He was a bit ago." He looked around as if he expected his brother to pop up from behind one of the desks. "I guess he went downstairs."

She tapped her foot. "I need to speak with him. Can you go downstairs and fetch him?"

Just then Dante entered the office. "What are you doing here, Diana?"

She sighed. "I came to see Hunt. Has he left?"

"Just a few minutes ago. I believe he was headed home."

An ache was beginning at the back of her head. As long as she'd come this far, she might as well finish her mission. "Fine. I will go to his house, thank you, Dante."

"I can escort you to your carriage."

She waved him off. "That's not necessary. I can find my way."

Once she reached the bottom step, she stopped and decided to peek into the gaming room. There was no point in coming this far and not assuaging her curiosity.

She approached the wooden door with a glass panel in the top and glanced through.

The room was amazing. Tables held men playing various card games. A bar lined one wall with several men leaning against it, drinking and observing the crowd. There were a few women, and obviously from their mode of dress and painted faces, not the respectable women of London. She smiled at being given the chance to see this.

On the other wall there was some sort of spinning wheel that men were shouting over, and a large table was surrounded by clients throwing dice and groaning.

She glanced to the east side of the building where three men sat at a table with another man standing in front of them dealing cards. Her eyes drifted up, she blinked a few times, then sucked in a deep breath.

It was not possible, and she was quite certain her eyes deceived her. Licking her dry lips, she pushed the door open and walked into the room.

One of the men who was obviously an employee came up to her. "I am sorry, my lady, you are not permitted on the gaming floor."

She pushed him aside and continued into the room. The blood pounded so hard in her head sounds grew dim and black dots danced in her eyes. She got as far as the wall and looked up.

With a soft sigh, Diana's eyes rolled to the back of her head, and she slid towards the floor.

22

Hunt ran his fingers through his hair for probably the hundredth time as he continued to pace in his library. A half empty brandy bottle sat on his desk, but he'd had enough to calm him down, but not to forget.

The damn portrait was hanging in The Rose Room!

Every time that thought entered his brain, he felt the need to punch the wall, or perhaps his brother. He again went over his conversation with Dante after discovering the painting.

He'd flown up the stairs, slammed into the office, and grabbed Dante by his cravat, lifting him off the chair. "Why the devil is that painting hanging on the wall downstairs?"

Driscoll was even surprised enough to look up from his work. "What the hell, Hunt. What's going on?"

He shook Dante and let him go, dropping him back into his chair. "You took that painting from my house."

His brother straightened his cravat. "I did you a favor."

Hunt fisted his hands on his hips. "What favor?"

Obviously, the look on Hunt's face disturbed his usually devil-may-care brother because he leaned back.

"You're married now. You don't need that kind of painting in your house. If your wife found it, she would probably shoot you." He snapped his fingers. "Ah, I'll bet she did see it and that's why you're so out of sorts."

"Keep my wife out of this." God, just mentioning Diana brought sweat to his brow. "Anyway, take it down, I'm taking it home."

"I don't think that's a good business move, brother," Driscoll said, pushing his glasses farther up on his nose. "Ever since that portrait was hung, we've had more crowds than usual. Word has spread, and everyone assumes the young lady is of the demimonde, and they are trying to guess who she is. I believe there is even a betting page."

Hunt felt as though he was punched in the stomach. His wife, the woman he loved more than anything in the world, was on display for the entire *ton* to ogle. The only thing keeping him from howling like a mad dog was the fact that Mallory got it wrong and that was not truly his wife's beautiful body on display.

"Do you have some particular interest in the woman, Hunt?" Dante asked. "Is she your former mistress?" He looked over at Driscoll. "All the more reason to have it out of your house."

Dear God, how to get out of this mess without letting them know it was his innocent wife who had been duped into that scandalous portrait? If he didn't calm down, his very smart brothers might go in a direction he had no intention of letting them wander. "No. She is not one of my mistresses."

"Who is she? If you give us a name, we can encourage even more bets," Dante said.

Hunt leaned toward his brother. "I want it taken down. Now."

Dante and Driscoll glanced at each other, and Hunt was not happy with the puzzled look they shared. He needed to back off and give himself time to deal with this. "Very well." He brushed the sleeves of his jacket. "I will leave now, but this is not over." He pointed his finger at Dante. "Don't ever take anything from my house again without my permission. I should call the magistrate and have you locked up."

With those words, he left the office, slamming the door hard enough that something fell from the wall and landed on the floor.

NOW HE LIVED in fear that somehow—he had no idea how—Diana would find out about this. He was certain that would be the end of their marriage. Would she even believe him if he told her he had nothing to do with where the painting rested now?

He walked to the brandy bottle and was pouring another when Dante came striding into the library. "Hunt, you have to come to the club. Diana just passed out."

Could this night get any worse? "What was Diana doing in the club?"

"Looking for you, but I told her you had gone home. She was headed out of the club when she collapsed."

He rubbed his hand over his face. Diana had gone to the club. There was only one reason why she would faint.

Hunt returned the bottle to the table and headed past Dante. It would be faster on his horse, but he couldn't sling Diana over his shoulder and ride her home through the streets of London like some pirate carrying his bounty. "Did you come in a carriage?" he asked Dante as he raced past a confused Peters.

"Yes. It's out front."

They climbed in after Hunt shouted at the driver to take whatever route would get them to the club fastest.

Once they settled in, Hunt glared at Dante. "Tell me what happened."

Dante shrugged. "Once I told her you had gone home, I offered to escort her to her carriage, but she declined—"

"—That was your second mistake," Hunt growled.

Apparently his brother did not have to wonder about his first mistake since a blush covered his face. "I left the office a couple of minutes later to see her opening the door to the gaming room. I tried to catch her as she wandered off, but people kept getting in my way. She walked almost the entire length of the room when she suddenly slid to the floor."

From what Dante had just told him, it didn't sound as though he noticed Diana looking up at the painting before she fainted. There was no doubt in his mind that her collapse had everything to do with seeing it.

Since there didn't seem to be anything else to say, silence reigned in the carriage until they reached The Rose Room. Hunt jumped from the vehicle and hurried up the steps to the front door. A quick knock, and the door opened.

"Where is my wife?" He asked Pomeroy, the guard at the door, as he pushed past him.

"Upstairs in the office."

Hunt nodded and made his way through the club and upstairs to the offices. He opened the door to see Diana sitting upright, a crumpled handkerchief in her hand. She looked over at him and immediately flew across the room. Hunt fought the desire to duck, but instead of tossing something at his head, or walloping him on the jaw, she threw herself into his arms.

* * *

As much as Diana wanted to throttle the man, she was so glad to see him. It was obvious from the conversation she'd had with both Driscoll and Dante that they had no idea the painting hanging on the wall downstairs was her. The look on Hunt's face, and the way he seemed to brace himself for a blow when he opened the door, told her he was not complicit.

His eyes seemed to devour her. He rubbed his palms over her arms, concern written all over his face and demeanor. "Are you all right, Diana?"

She shook her head. "Not at all. But I feel well enough to go home. I think we have a lot to talk about."

Dante eyed her up and down, then turned to Hunt. "I don't think she harmed herself. Luckily I was close enough to catch her when she fainted, so she didn't reach the floor."

"Thank you for that, Dante." Hunt was unusually annoyed with his brother, but she was still reeling from the shock she'd received and pushed the thought aside.

They said their goodbyes to Driscoll and Dante and left in silence. Hunt kept his arm wrapped around her waist, hugging her body close to his. She certainly needed the support, just the thought of her portrait hanging in The Rose Room made her knees weak.

She looked around as they left the building. "Where is your carriage?"

"I came in Dante's carriage. I'll send it back once we're home." He waved the driver forward.

The vehicle rolled to a stop in front of them, and Diana leaned against the seat, feeling drained, like a rag doll. Although Hunt studied her carefully, he didn't say a word, and she wondered if he was waiting for her to pull out a pistol and shoot him.

"I might have planned a slow and horrible death for you when I first awoke from my faint, but given your attitude, it's apparent to me you had nothing to do with my portrait gracing the walls of The Rose Room."

Hunt sucked in a breath. "Of course not! I was appalled when I saw it. In fact, I still owe my youngest brother a sound thrashing."

"Ah, so he is the scoundrel in this bad play?" She

closed her eyes, hoping the headache that she'd awoken to would leave her. It was hard to think when in pain. "Why don't you tell me how this all came about? I'm too tired to argue about it."

Hunt cleared his throat. "You left the portrait in my library. I had instructed Peters to take it somewhere far away and burn the damn thing and not return until it was in ashes."

She opened her eyes and glared at him. "Then he would see the painting."

He shook his head. "As noted before, your face is turned in such a way that unless you are standing right next to it in a very bright light, no one can tell it is you. I'm sure Peters thought it was a painting of a past paramour that I wanted to be rid of before you saw it."

"How did it get in The Rose Room?"

"My idiot brother came to my house, for I don't know what when I was out, saw the painting, assumed it was something I wanted to get rid of for the same reason I imagine Peters did, and decided to 'save' me, as he said, from you seeing it."

"So, instead, the male population of the *ton* got to see it." She paused for a moment. "If you had only burned it like I asked. . ." She sighed and turned her head to look out at the darkness. "Why didn't you demand they take it down?"

"Because, once I began to make demands, Driscoll and Dante started to look at me strangely. I did *not* want them to figure out it was you."

She sucked in a deep breath. "Oh, God, no!"

The carriage rolled to a stop in front of their townhouse. Hunt dismissed the driver back to The Rose Room and escorted Diana into the house.

"Good evening, my lord, my lady." Peters bowed as they entered.

"Good evening Peters," Diana said with a smile. "Will you please have tea and a light repast sent up to our bedchamber?" As they climbed the stairs, she said, "I have the beginnings of a headache, and tea and a little food oftentimes helps."

Once they were in Hunt's bedchamber behind closed doors, Diana pulled off her gloves, dropped them onto the dressing table, and sat on the bed. "I had great plans to have you groveling at my feet, you know."

"I deserve it, sweetheart. The last thing I ever wanted to do was hurt you. And yes, you can trust me." He walked to where she sat and took her hands, kneeling in front of her.

She smirked. "Is this the grovel?"

"Whatever you want from me to make it up to you, I will do." He kissed her knuckles. "I don't want to lose you, Diana. I love you and have probably always loved you."

Her brows rose. "You thought me a nuisance your whole life."

"No. I've been doing some serious thinking, and I realize the reason I kept pushing you away was because I was scared. A marriage to you will not be the calm, very boring one I had imagined all my life."

She shook her head with a slight laugh. "No, Hunt. No one has ever accused me of being boring." She leaned in and kissed him gently on the lips. "I love you too, even though you are a cad."

He climbed up alongside her just as a tap on the door announced the arrival of their tea. Hunt hopped up and allowed Peters to enter with a tray. The butler placed the tea and small sandwiches on the table, bowed, and offered Hunt a wink.

Hunt pulled Diana up from the bed. "Come, my love. Let's eat and then go to bed. It's been a long day."

Diana walked with him to the comfortable chair in front of the fire. "One thing as yet we have to decide on."

"What's that?" Hunt said as he poured tea for them both.

She stirred her tea and took a sip. "When are we going to break into The Rose Room and steal the portrait?"

23

Again, Hunt found himself dressed in all black to steal the same damn portrait. Only this time, like Melrose's house, Diana would be right beside him. He had a feeling she insisted on coming along to assure herself that the blasted thing was burned.

"These trousers are much too big." Diana entered his bedchamber from the sitting room between their rooms, her hands clutching the gathered waistline. "I'll need something to hold them up."

One look at her fine figure outlined by the trousers was enough for him to want to forget the plan and take her to bed. "I have a pair of braces you may use." He walked to the dresser and pulled out a pair. "Here, try this."

She grinned and held them up, dangling from her fingers. "Um, what do I do with these?"

Hunt took them from her hand. Who would have known he would have to act as valet for his wife? But then again, he played lady's maid to her on their honeymoon. He quickly fastened them then placed his hands on her shoulders and studied her, his eyes eating up all her curves. "You will never pass for a man, if that is your intended ploy."

She shook her head. "No. I just don't think a dress would be convenient attire for thievery."

It was close to four in the morning and, since The Rose Room closed at three, they were allowing time for the last of the gamers to leave and his brothers to indulge in their nightly wind-down brandies in the office. By the time he and Diana arrived, all should be quiet and empty.

At least he would be able to enter the club using his key, instead of breaking into the place.

Even though he expected no trouble, he stopped at the library first and took one of his pistols out of the case and tucked it into his pocket.

"Surely you don't plan to shoot one of your brothers?" Diana looked at him with horror.

"No, my love. But it is always safer when one is out and about London late at night to have protection."

To keep from startling the servants, they left through the back door. Their carriage awaited them, since there was no reason this time to avoid his vehicle being noticed. He had every right to be at the club. Even if it was after it closed.

As they made their way to The Rose Room, he thought about the portrait and how it had brought him and Diana together. Would he have changed his mind about her had he not seen her in the nude? That had certainly put her into a whole new light.

However, for as much as he'd been obsessed with lust for her once he'd seen the painting, now that he'd viewed her in the flesh, the portrait did nothing for him. Mallory did get it all wrong and his painting did not compare to Diana in the flesh, soft and warm and cuddled next to him.

With very little traffic on the streets, the carriage arrived quickly. "Even though we're not illegally entering the building, I still prefer to go through the back door."

He led her down the alleyway to the rear of the building. Using his key, he opened the door and they entered. "I am going to put on a few lights to help. If anyone from the Watch sees us, there is nothing wrong with one of the owners wandering the club after it's closed."

The place always looked so different when cast in dark shadows. The gaming tables resembled monsters waiting to pounce on a poor soul to grab and haul one to some evil place. The smell of whiskey and cheroots surrounded them as they wove their way around the tables.

"It looks quite different when empty," Diana said in a whisper.

Hunt nodded and took her hand to lead her to the wall where the portrait hung. He picked up one of the oil lamps from a table to carry with him.

"I think when we get to the portrait, the best way to do this is for you to climb onto my shoulders. That should make you tall enough to pluck the painting off the wall. Just be careful that it doesn't throw you off balance."

Diana nodded.

They arrived at the wall, and Hunt held up the oil lamp.

They both stared at the empty space where the portrait hung only hours before.

He turned to Diana, who looked back at him, both of their jaws slack.

"Where is the portrait?" they said at the same time.

"Oh, the devil take it," Diana said, apparently not too concerned about her language at this point. "Do you think your brother sold it? Do you think one of the patrons won it? Didn't I hear there was some sort of betting going on?" Her shaky voice rose higher and higher with each question until Hunt was certain she was working herself into a full-blown panic.

"Calm down, sweetheart. I don't know why they took it off the wall, but I'm sure it's in the office upstairs." He took her ice-cold hand. "Come."

It had better be in the office upstairs. He couldn't imagine why it would not be. He didn't even want to consider Diana's concerns about someone from the club winning it. He told himself the sweat that broke out on his body was from the exertion of climbing the steps to the office and not abject terror at that possibility.

He flung the door open, and they entered, lighting all the lamps as they wandered the space.

"I don't see it." Diana's voice was a dejected whisper.

They searched the office, as well as the supply room next to it. No portrait.

Hunt ran his hand down his face and then held his hand out to Diana. "Let's go."

"Where are we going?"

"To my brother's house so I can kill him."

"You can't go to Dante's house to kill him this late. He's probably sleeping."

"Good, then he won't know what hit him." He dragged her along the corridor, down the steps, and out the door. He just about tossed her into the carriage, slammed the door, and slumped in the corner of the vehicle.

* * *

DIANA'S STOMACH was in knots, but she still didn't think they should barge into Dante's house. He would certainly question their anxiety to get the painting back and might come up with an answer she definitely did not want.

She reached across the space between them and placed her hand over Hunt's. "Let's just go home. I'm tired, annoyed, and ready for a large brandy."

His brows rose. “Brandy? You? I’ve never seen you drink brandy before.”

She sighed. “If there ever was a time for me to start, I believe this is it.”

They remained silent for the ride home. Diana was indeed tired, actually bordering on exhaustion. She hadn’t slept in almost twenty-four hours, and she didn’t have the strength to worry about where the portrait was now.

If Mallory wasn’t already dead, she would shoot him herself.

It was a sorry, dejected pair who entered the town-house in Mayfair. The servants were already up and taking care of their chores when Diana and Hunt arrived home. The aroma of fresh baked bread filled the air, making her stomach rumble.

Hunt regarded her carefully. “Are you sure you want a brandy? Maybe tea and some food instead?”

Truthfully, the idea of brandy did turn her stomach, and the thought of tea and food appealed much more. “Yes. Thank you. That sounds much better, but you go ahead and have a brandy if you want one.”

“Why don’t you go to the kitchen and have Cook send breakfast to our room? We can eat and then sleep before we decide what our next step is.”

Diana wandered to the kitchen, Cook’s eyes growing wide at Diana’s attire and early appearance.

“May I help you, my lady?”

“Yes. His lordship and I were out, and we would like our breakfast sent up to our bedchamber as soon as it is ready.”

“Yes, of course.” As a good employee, Cook turned and began pulling items from the larder. Most likely, after years of working for the nobility, she had learned to expect anything at all.

“Diana!” Hunt’s shout had her hurrying from the

kitchen to the library. Hunt stood with a glass of brandy in his hand, staring at a spot behind his desk.

"What is it?"

He turned to her and grinned. "The portrait."

"What?" Diana rounded the desk and looked down. There, leaning against the wall, sat the portrait. She turned to Hunt. "How?"

He shook his head. "The only idea I have is Dante took it down and returned it. Most likely on his way home from the club. He probably passed us on the street as we headed to The Rose Room."

"I wonder why?"

Hunt took the final sip of his drink and placed the glass on the desk. "Most likely because I made such a fuss over it."

"So now you won't kill him?" Diana asked as she flipped the linen back over the painting.

"No. I've oftentimes wondered how someone as intelligent as Dante could be at times as dumb as a rock." He shook his head. "Is breakfast on the way?"

"Yes." She reached out and took Hunt's hand and they wearily climbed the stairs together. "Maybe we can think of something to do that will keep us awake before breakfast arrives." She smirked at her husband who smirked back.

"Yes, my love. I'm sure there is something."

TWO DAYS LATER, Hunt loaded a picnic basket, a bottle of wine, and the cursed portrait into his open-air carriage. He turned to help Diana in, then strode to the other side of the vehicle and hopped in. "Ready?"

"Yes. More than ready," Diana responded as she twirled her parasol on her shoulder.

The day was warm and pleasant, with the sun bright in the sky. They were headed to a spot far outside of London where the air was fresher and more agreeable.

Dante had stopped by their house on his way to work the afternoon they had returned to find the portrait in the library. He'd been very apologetic and asked their forgiveness for taking the painting without permission.

Frankly, she did not like the way he looked at her, which led her to believe he knew the painting was her. Hunt must have thought that also since he told Dante they were never to speak of the portrait again, and he must erase it from his mind. He also instructed him to tell Driscoll the same thing. Dante managed to keep the smile off his face, but everything about his demeanor told her he knew.

After about a thirty-minute ride with them chatting about their return soon to Hunt's country estate, they arrived at a lovely spot with trees surrounding a grassy area next to a brook. "This is beautiful," Diana said.

"Yes. I've never stopped here but passed it many times. I think this is perfect for our purpose."

Diana spread the blanket on the soft warm grass while Hunt unloaded the portrait and the basket. Cook had sent cold meat, cheese, bread, and apples. Hunt poured the wine.

Once they finished, Hunt searched the ground for small kindling sticks, which he made into a pile. He lit a few sticks, blew on the pile, and once he had the fire going well, he threw on larger pieces of wood.

And then, finally, the painting.

They'd taken it out of the frame which they'd given to one of the servants, and then sat back against a tree, watching the portrait burn while they finished the wine.

Once the portrait was burned beyond recognition, Hunt cupped Diana's chin and turned her face toward him. "Only one more thing will make this trip perfect."

Diana felt her heartbeat pick up and flutters in her stomach. "What is that?" she whispered.

"I think it's time we made love outdoors." He nuzzled her neck. "This is a very isolated place and, if we walk farther into the wooded area behind us, we will be invisible."

"Is that right, my lord?"

He grinned and stood, reaching out for her hand. She accepted and, with their arms wrapped around each other's waists, they made their way into the cool forest area.

They didn't return for quite some time.

EPILOGUE

Nine months later
London, England

"Hunt, I really prefer to have this baby at our country estate. I can't help but think the air and noise is not good for either of us." Diana shifted in her chair, attempting to get comfortable. Comfort near the end of one's pregnancy was generally hard to find, she'd discovered.

"Darling, we've been over this," Hunt said as he scanned the newspaper. "The best doctor is right here in London, and I want the best for you and the baby."

"Ha. I believe you're telling yourself that because you want to be here for Parliament, so you can meet with all your friends and pretend you're serving the country."

Hunt lowered the newspaper and stared at his wife. With messy curls hanging from her topknot and the scowl on her face, she looked like an adorable toddler annoyed at not having her own way. He couldn't help but grin.

"Don't laugh at me!"

'I'm sorry, sweetheart. I don't mean to laugh, it's just

that you know in your heart Dr. Reading is the best doctor in London for delivering healthy and happy babies. You selected him yourself."

"I know." She shifted again. "I do need to get out of the house. I hate that a pregnant woman out and about is scandalous."

Hunt folded the newspaper and placed it alongside his empty breakfast plate. "We shall go out, then."

"Really?" Her eyes reflected the joy in his statement, causing a bit of guilt to rest in his chest. He had been spending too much time on business and Parliament, neglecting his beautiful wife who was growing close to her time to give birth.

"Yes. I shall order the carriage brought around, and we will take a leisurely ride around Hyde Park. Then we will make a stop at Gunter's and order ices brought to our carriage. How does that sound?"

"Wonderful!"

He groaned inwardly when tears pooled in her eyes. She'd been so prone to bouts of weepiness of late that he always had a handkerchief at the ready. Which he promptly removed from his pocket and handed to her.

"Thank you." She patted the corners of her eyes. "When shall I be ready?"

"I think after luncheon. The air will be warmer so the ices don't freeze us to death."

"Well, look who's still lollygagging at the breakfast table. Don't you have work to do?" Dante entered the breakfast room, Driscoll right behind him. "At least that's what you always tell me when I'm on a well-deserved break at the club."

His brothers pulled out chairs and sat. Dante reached for a slice of toast and the jar of jam to top it with. "How is my favorite sister-in-law feeling today?"

"Tired. Bored. Ready to have the baby." She smiled at the two men who had made almost as much a fuss over her as Hunt did.

"I do have work, in fact. I have to check over the financial statements you sent me," Hunt said.

"Ah, don't trust your own flesh and blood, eh?" Driscoll took an orange from the middle of the table and began to peel it.

Hunt grew serious. He loved these two men and would trust them with his and his wife's lives. "I trust you, as you well know. But mistakes happen."

"Lately there seems to be a lot of mistakes coming from Miss Pence's table," Dante said and glanced over at Driscoll. Despite trying to look indifferent, there was a slight blush to Driscoll's face.

"I'm sure everything is fine."

"*Miss* Pence? You have a woman working at The Rose Room?"

"Yes, and her table is swarmed every night," Dante said between bites.

Hunt looked over at Driscoll who was in charge of hiring. "Whatever made you hire a woman?"

"She's smart, talented, a good worker and the members love her." His words were clipped as if expecting Hunt to challenge him.

Hunt shrugged. "Your decision." He looked at Dante. "What is the problem with her table?"

"Nothing," Driscoll said as Dante also answered, "Could be shortages."

"Well, I will leave you gentlemen to fight this out. I am going to take a short lie-down before Hunt and I go for our ride this afternoon." Diana rose, and all three brothers jumped to their feet.

"Are you well, Diana? You look a little drawn." Hunt studied her as he rounded the table to take her arm.

"I'm fine. Just a bit tired, as I said. I also have been troubled by a backache all night."

"Should I send for Dr. Reading?" Hunt frowned as he led her out of the breakfast room.

"No."

He helped her upstairs and called for Marguerite to assist her in undressing so she could rest comfortably.

Diana grabbed his arm as he made to leave the room. "We're still going on our ride this afternoon, correct?"

"If you feel up to it, sweeting."

"I will. I promise."

He kissed her on the head and returned to the breakfast room where his brothers were in the midst of an argument.

"Are you two still arguing about Miss Pence?"

"There is nothing wrong with Miss Pence's final tally reports." Driscoll practically growled at Dante.

Dante shrugged. "If you say so."

"How did you find this female dealer?" Hunt motioned to the footman to bring another pot of coffee.

"She fell in his lap," Dante said, grinning widely.

Driscoll made to jump up and swing at his brother. Hunt grabbed the back of Driscoll's jacket. "Knock it off. What's the matter with the two of you?"

"Hunt!"

The scream from their bedchamber had Hunt forgetting all about his brothers and racing up the stairs. Marguerite met him, wringing her hands. "Her waters have broken, my lord."

"What?" He had no idea what the maid was talking about. "Did she spill a glass of water on herself? Is that why she's wailing in there?" He gestured with his thumb at the door and the sound of Diana crying.

Again.

"No, my lord. Her waters have broken. You must send for Dr. Reading."

"Well, why didn't you say so, instead of talking about spilled water?" He thundered down the stairs to the front door. "Peters, send for Dr. Reading. I think Lady Huntington is having the baby."

He turned to see Dante and Driscoll striding toward the door. "I think this is a good time for us to take our leave." Driscoll pounded him on his back. "Let us know when it is all over."

Like two scurrying lads in trouble with the headmaster, the brothers grabbed their hats from Peters and fled the house.

"Hunt!" Another cry from upstairs.

Hunt gave Peters a shove to his shoulder. "Go. Get the doctor."

Then he hurried back upstairs. Marguerite was just leaving the bedchamber, holding some wet clothing. "How is she?"

"Frightened, my lord. She's never done this before."

"Me, either," he mumbled as he passed the maid and entered the room.

"I've sent for Dr. Reading, my love." He sat alongside her on the bed and held her hand. "He will be here shortly."

She nodded, then gripped his hands as her face twisted in pain. Blasted hell, he wanted to be anywhere but here. He hated watching his wife suffer and not able to do anything about it.

The next two hours passed with Diana alternating between squeezing his hand and panting and chattering non-stop about the baby and where the hell was Dr. Reading?

The same question he had. He tried twice to go back downstairs and pummel someone into hurrying up, but Diana would not let him leave.

Finally, they heard the sound of footsteps and the gruff voice of Dr. Reading. He entered the room right behind Marguerite. "Ah, here is our patient. I knew it was growing close to your time." He turned to Marguerite. "My assistant is right behind me in another carriage with the necessary supplies. Can you have a footman assist her?"

"Yes, Doctor."

Dr. Reading waved Hunt off. "Young man, it appears you've already done your work, now it's time for your wife to take over and bring this bundle of joy into the world."

Hunt hated how relieved he was to be dismissed. He should be strong and stay here with Diana, but he was in dire need of a brandy. Especially since her whimpers had turned into downright screams in the past half-hour. Mostly at him.

"I will be downstairs, Doctor, if you need me for anything."

The doctor nodded and turned his attention to Diana.

Hunt never left a room so fast in his life. He sure as hell didn't mind doing his part at the beginning of this blessed event, but the end result was best left to women and doctors.

Nine hours later, he was still pacing the library. He'd waved off luncheon and had only a bite of dinner before sending it back to the kitchen. There were a great deal of cuss words coming from his innocent and well-bred wife. Where she'd even heard some of them was questionable. More than a few were in Italian, but he didn't have to speak the language to know she wasn't praising him.

God, as annoying as his brothers could be, he wished they were here with him. He no sooner got the thought composed in his head when the library door opened, and the two miscreants entered.

"We couldn't let you do this alone. Once we were sure the club was set to go tonight, we left Keniel in charge."

"Who?"

"The new manager. From Jamaica. His name is Keniel Singh. Pleasant chap, but there's something familiar about him, although he says he's never been to England before."

The three took turns pacing, assuring each other all was well, and grimacing each time Diana spewed a curse aimed at her husband. His two brothers looked at him with sympathy.

"Do you think she will ever let you near her bed again?" Dante asked with apparent sincerity.

"I'm not sure I ever want her in my bed again." Hunt ran his fingers through his hair. "This is brutal."

Unexpectedly, another scream erupted from the room upstairs, but this one sounded very much like a very small human. A not very happy human.

"The babe?" Hunt said, a slight grin on his face.

Marguerite came bounding down the stairs and hustled into the library. "My lord, come quickly."

Hunt's heart dropped to his stomach. "Is Diana all right?"

"Yes, yes, she's fine. Come and see your daughter."

Hunt turned to his brothers, knowing the silly grin on his face would be brought up many times over the years. "I have a daughter."

They slapped him on the back. "Well done, man."

"Don't let Diana hear you say that. She's done all the work." He headed up the stairs. "I will summon you when my wife is respectable."

Hunt slowly opened the door to see Diana holding a little bundle who had quieted down somewhat. Marguerite had cleaned his wife up. She wore a fresh nightgown, her hair had been brushed, and a ribbon held it back at her nape. She looked up. "Come, Hunt. Come see our daughter."

She acted as though everything was quite normal after he'd spent hours listening to her suffering and cursing him.

He sat next to her on the bed, his insides shaking like

jelly. "A little girl." Blonde fuzz covered her tiny head. She looked so fragile, so helpless. A sense of protection he'd never felt before, not even for his beloved wife, swamped him, almost bringing him to his knees.

He reached out with a shaky finger and touched the extremely soft skin on her face. "She looks like you."

"I know. I hope she is just like me, too." She grinned at him, her eyes teasing. "Don't you?"

Good heavens, no. I will be bald from snatching out my hair by the time the urchin is ten years.

"Of course, my love, of course. Just like you." He leaned over and kissed Diana's lips. "Just like you."

He was amazed to realize he meant it.

The End

Did you like this story? Please consider leaving a review on either Goodreads or the place where you bought it. Long or short, your review will help other readers discover new authors and make purchasing decisions!

I hope you had fun reading Diana and Hunt's love story. For more Rose Room Rogue romance, read *A Lady's Trust.*

Driscoll Rose and his two brothers own and run The Rose Room, a well-known and profitable gaming club in London. Unknown to those who visit and spend their money there, the brothers also work for the Crown in positions only known to a mysterious man at the Home Office.

Miss Amelia Pence is on the run from her step-brother who has nefarious plans for her. Late one rainy night she crawls into Driscoll's office window and falls at his feet. Intrigued by the woman, he offers her a job as the only female dealer in the Rose Room.

Amelia is secretive about who she is, and where she lives since she can trust no one, much to Driscoll's frustration. The growing attraction between them and his desire for her is causing him to dismiss the fact that crowds of gamblers swarm her table each evening, but the profits she turns in are not what they should be.

Want to read the rest of the story? Visit my website: http://calliehutton.com/book/a-ladys-trust/

You can find a list of all my books on my website: http://calliehutton.com/books/

ABOUT THE AUTHOR

Receive a free book and stay up to date with new releases and sales!
http://calliehutton.com/newsletter/

USA Today bestselling author, Callie Hutton, has penned more than 45 historical romance and cozy mystery books. She lives in Oklahoma with her very close and lively family, which includes her twin grandsons, affectionately known as "The Twinadoes."

Callie loves to hear from readers. Contact her directly at calliehutton11@gmail.com or find her online at www.calliehutton.com.

Connect with her on Facebook, Twitter, and Goodreads. Follow her on BookBub to receive notice of new releases, preorders, and special promotions.

Praise for books by Callie Hutton

A Study in Murder

"This book is a delight!...*A Study in Murder* has clear echoes of Jane Austen, Agatha Christie, and of course, Sherlock Holmes. You will love this book." —William Bernhardt, author of *The Last Chance Lawyer*

"A one-of-a-kind new series that's packed with surprises." —Mary Ellen Hughes, National bestselling author of *A Curio Killing*.

"[A] lively and entertaining mystery...I predict a long run for this smart series." —Victoria Abbott, award-winning author of The Book Collector Mysteries

"With a breezy style and alluring, low-keyed humor, Hutton crafts a charming mystery with a delightful, irrepressible sleuth." —Madeline Hunter, *New York Times* bestselling author of *Never Deny a Duke*

The Elusive Wife

"I loved this book and you will too. Jason is a hottie & Oliva is the kind of woman we'd all want as a friend. Read it!" —Cocktails and Books

"In my experience I've had a few hits but more misses with historical romance so I was really pleasantly surprised to be hooked from the start by obviously good writing." —Book Chick City

"The historic elements and sensory details of each scene make the story come to life, and certainly helps immerse the reader in the world that Olivia and Jason share." —The Romance Reviews

"You will not want to miss *The Elusive Wife*." —My Book Addiction

"...it was a well written plot and the characters were likeable." —Night Owl Reviews

A Run for Love

"An exciting, heart-warming Western love story!" —*New York Times* bestselling author Georgina Gentry

"I loved this book!!! I read the BEST historical romance last night...It's called *A Run For Love*." —*New York Times* bestselling author Sharon Sala

"This is my first Callie Hutton story, but it certainly won't be my last." —The Romance Reviews

An Angel in the Mail

"...a warm fuzzy sensuous read. I didn't put it down until I was done." —Sizzling Hot Reviews

Visit www.calliehutton.com for more information.

Made in the USA
Las Vegas, NV
04 July 2021

25916907R00120